The Sanctuary and Twenty-Three Hundred Days

By

Elder J. N. Andrews.

"Unto two thousand and three hundred days,
then shall the sanctuary be cleansed."
Dan. 8:14.

TEACH Services, Inc.
P U B L I S H I N G
www.TEACHServices.com

Copyright © 1997, 2012 TEACH Services, Inc.
ISBN-13: 978-0-945383-84-0 (Paperback)
ISBN-13: 978-1-57258-967-4 (ePub)
ISBN-13: 978-1-57258-810-0 (Kindle)
Library of Congress Control Number: 97-60846

Published by

TEACH Services, Inc.

P U B L I S H I N G

www.TEACHServices.com

Table of Contents

Introduction

NO apology can be needed for the presentation of this subject. Those who have any interest in the past Advent movement, cannot be otherwise than deeply interested in the question of our disappointment. To examine this question with candor and fairness, and to set forth the reasons why our expectations were not realized, is the object of this work.

Several points presented in these pages may, however, need to be briefly noticed. On pages 30 and 31, we quoted from the *Advent Herald* a denial of the connection between the 70 weeks and 2300 days by S. Bliss. But justice to Elder Himesdemands that we here state that in a recent number of the *Herald* he has acknowledged their connection. Referring to the first lecture which he heard Mr. Miller deliver, he remarks:

"He poured forth a flood of light from other scriptures upon every part of his subject, and fully shut me up to the faith, both as to the *manner* and time of our Saviour's second advent. And although the time has passed without thee vent being realized, I have never been able to solve the mystery. The connection of the seventy weeks with the 2300 days' vision still looks clear, but it cannot be harmonized with the *light* we now have on chronology; but having done our duty, we wait patiently for the clear light of Heaven upon the subject, in expectation of the full and speedy [3] realization of all we ever hoped for in the fulfillment of prophecy, both as to the nature of the events,

5

and the time of their realization, at the end of the days. And we are exhorted, in view of this, not to 'cast away our confidence, which hath great recompense of reward, for we have need of patience, that after we have done the will of God, we might receive the promise.' So we watch, and wait, and hope" (*Advent Herald*, Feb. 26, 1853).

That this subject should be shrouded in mystery to those who believe that the earth is the sanctuary, is not strange; for if the connection between the 70 weeks and the 2300 days be admitted, it is certain that the period has ended. And if the earth is the sanctuary, the prophecy has failed; for no part of the earth has as yet undergone a change. Hence, there is no way to explain the passing of the time, unless we deny the connection of the 70 weeks and the 2300 days, or conclude that the earth may not be the sanctuary. The first of these positions is adopted by S. Bliss. Elder H., however, still admits the connection of the two periods, but contents himself with calling our disappointment a mystery.

But does the Bible call the earth the sanctuary? Does it warrant the conclusion that at the end of the period the earth would be burned? Does it not, on the contrary, by a mass of testimony, teach that something else is the sanctuary of the Lord? And does it not also teach a different method of cleansing the sanctuary than by fire? The answer to these questions will be found in the following pages:

On pages 67-70 the prophecy of Ezekiel (chaps. 40-48) respecting the restoration of the typical [4] sanctuary is noticed. The position is there taken that those blessings were offered to Israel on certain conditions, and that they belonged to the period of the typical dispensation. And further, that, as these conditions were never complied with, the promised blessings were never bestowed upon that people. The reasons for this view are there presented. The following from *Bliss' Commentary on the Apocalypse*, pages 7 and 8, may be of value to the reader:

6

"CONDITIONAL PROPHECY is when the fulfillment is dependent on the compliance of those to whom the promise is made, with the conditions on which it is given. *Examples*: 'If ye walk in my statutes, and keep my commandments, and do them; then I will give you rain in due season, and the land shall yield her increase, and the trees of the field shall yield her fruit.' Lev. 26:3, 4 'But *if* ye will *not* hearken unto me, and will *not* do all these commandments; and *if* ye shall despise my statutes, or if your soul abhor my judgments, so that ye will not do all my commandments, *but* that ye break my covenant; I also will do this unto you: I will even appoint over you terror, consumption, and the burning ague, that shall consume the eyes, and cause sorrow of heart; and ye shall sow your seed in vain; for your enemies shall eat it.' Verses 14-16. 'And it shall come to pass, *if* thou shalt hearken diligently unto the voice of the Lord thy God, to observe and to do all his commandments which I command thee this day, that the Lord thy God will set thee on high above all nations of the earth; and all these blessings shall come on thee, and overtake thee, *if* thou shalt hearken unto the voice of the Lord thy God.' [5] Deut. 28:1, 2 'But it shall come to pass, *if* thou wilt not hearken unto the voice of the Lord thy God, to observe to do all his commandments and his statutes which I command thee this day; that all these curses shall come upon thee, and overtake thee, ' etc. Verse 15.

"Predictions of mere national prosperity, or adversity, are usually conditional. When the condition is not expressed, it is implied.

"*Example*—The Lord said unto Jonah, 'Arise, go unto Nineveh, that great city, and preach unto it the preaching that I bid thee. * * And Jonah began to enter into the city a day's journey, and he cried, and said, Yet forty days, and Nineveh shall be overthrown. So the people of Nineveh believed God, and proclaimed a fast, and put on sackcloth, from the greatest of them even to the least of them. * *And God saw

7

their works, that they turned from their evil way; and God repented of the evil, that he had said that he would do unto them; and he did it not.'

"For all cases of this kind, the Lord has given the following general RULE: 'At what instant I shall speak concerning a nation, and concerning a kingdom, to pluck up, and to pull down, and to destroy it; if that nation, against whom I have pronounced, turn from their evil, I will repent of the evil that I thought to do unto them. And at what instant I shall speak concerning a nation, and concerning a kingdom, to build and to plant it; if it do evil in my sight, that it obey not my voice, then I will repent of the good, wherewith I said I would benefit them.' Jer. 18:7-10."

J.N.A.[6]

The Sanctuary

I N presenting this most important subject for the consideration of the people of God, we invite the candid and prayerful attention of all who have ears to hear. It is well understood by thousands that the great disappointment of the Advent believers arose from the fact that they believed the cleansing of the sanctuary to be the burning of the earth, or some event to transpire at the second advent of the Lord Jesus; and as they could clearly establish the fact that the 2300 days would terminate in the autumn of 1844, they looked with the full assurance of faith and hope for the glorious appearing of the Son of God at that time. Painful and grievous was the disappointment;and while the heart of the trusting was bowed with sorrow, numbers were not wanting who openly denied the hand of God in the Advent movement, and made utter shipwreck of their faith.

As the subject of the sanctuary of the Bible involves the most important facts connected with our disappointment, it is worthy of the serious attention of all who wait the consolation of Israel. Let us then examine again with care the vision of the man greatly beloved, recorded in Daniel 8. We call attention to the symbols presented in this chapter. The first thing presented to the eye of the prophet, was:

THE VIEW OF THE RAM—"Then I lifted up mine eyes, and saw, and behold, there stood [7] before the river a ram which had two horns; and the two horns were high; but one was higher than the other, and the higher came up last. I saw the ram pushing westward, and northward, and southward; so that no beasts might stand before him, neither was there any that could deliver out of his hand; but he did according to his will, and became great" (Verses 3, 4).

THE VIEW OF THE GOAT—"And as I was considering, behold an he goat came from the west on the face of the whole earth, and touched not the ground; and the goat had a notable horn between his eyes. And he came to the ram that had two horns, which I had seen standing before the river, and ran unto him in the fury of his power. And I saw him come close unto the ram, and he was moved with choler against him, and smote the ram, and brake his two horns;and there was no power in the ram to stand before him, but he cast him down to the ground, and stamped upon him; and there was none that could deliver the ram out of his hand. Therefore, the he goat waxed very great; and when he was strong, the great horn was broken; and for it, came up four notable ones toward the four winds of heaven" (Verses 5-8).

THE VIEW OF THE LITTLE HORN—"And out of one of them came forth a little horn, which waxed exceeding great, toward the south, and toward the east, and toward the pleasant land. And it waxed great, even to the host of heaven; and it cast down some of the host and of the stars to the ground, and stamped upon them. Yea, he magnified himself even to the Prince of the host, and by him the daily sacrifice was taken away, and the place of his sanctuary was cast down. And [8] an host was given him against the daily sacrifice by reason of transgression, and it cast down the truth to the ground; and it practiced, and prospered" (Verses 9-12).

THE VIEW OF THE SANCTUARY AND 2300 DAYS—"Then I heard one saint speaking, and another saint said unto that certain saint which spake, How long shall be the vision, concerning the daily sacrifice, and transgression of desolation, to give both the sanctuary

10

and the host to be trodden under foot? And he said unto me, Unto 2300 days; then shall the sanctuary be cleansed" (Verses 13, 14).

Gabriel Commanded
to Explain this Vision

A ND it came to pass, when I, even I Daniel, had seen the vision, and sought for the meaning, then behold there stood before me as the appearance of a man. And I heard a man's voice between the banks of Ulai, which called, and said, Gabriel, make this man to understand the vision. So he came near where I stood; and when he came, I was afraid, and fell upon my face; but he said unto me, Understand, O son of man; for at the time of the end shall be the vision. Now as he was speaking with me, I was in a deep sleep on my face toward the ground; but he touched me and set me upright. And he said, Behold, I will make thee know what shall be in the last end of the indignation; for at the time appointed the end shall be" (Verses 15-19).

SYMBOL OF THE RAM EXPLAINED.—"The ram which thou sawest having two horns are the kings of Media and Persia" (Verse 20). Then the [9] meaning of the first symbol cannot be misunderstood. By it, the Medo-Persian Empire was presented to the eye of the prophet; its two horns denoting the union of these two powers in one government. This vision, therefore, does not begin with the empire of Babylon, as do the visions of the second and seventh chapters, but it commences with the empire of the Medes and Persians at the right of its power, prevailing westward, northward, and southward, so that no power could stand before it. The explanation of the next symbol will show what power overthrew the Persian Empire and succeeded to its place.

SYMBOLS OF THE GOAT EXPLAINED—"And the rough goat is the king of Grecia; and the great horn that is between his eyes is the first king. Now that being broken, whereas four stood up for it, four kingdoms shall stand up out of the nation, but not in his power" (Verses 21, 22). The explanation of this symbol is also definite and certain. The power that should overthrow the Medes and Persians, and in their stead, bear rule over the earth, is the empire of the Greeks. Greece succeeded Persia in the dominion of the world B.C. 331. The great horn is here explained to be the first king of Grecia; it was Alexander the Great. The four horns that arose when this horn was broken, denote the four kingdoms into which the empire of Alexander was divided after his death. The same was presented by the four heads and four wings of the leopard (Dan. 7:6). It is predicted without the use of symbols in Dan. 11:3, 4. These four kingdoms were Macedon, Thrace, Syria, and Egypt. They originated B.C. 312. [10]

SYMBOL OF THE LITTLE HORN EXPLAINED—"And in the latter time of their kingdom, when the transgressors are come to the full, a king of fierce countenance, and understanding dark sentences, shall stand up. And his power shall be mighty, but not by his own power; and he shall destroy wonderfully, and shall prosper, and practice, and shall destroy the mighty and the holy people. And through his policy also he shall cause craft to prosper in his hand;and he shall magnify himself in his heart, and by peace shall destroy many; he shall also stand up against the Prince of princes; but he shall be broken without hand" (Verses 23-25).

To avoid the application of this prophecy to the Roman power, pagan and papal, the papists have shifted it from Rome to Antiochus Epiphanes, a Syrian king *who could not resist* the mandates of Rome. See notes of the Douay (Romish) Bible on Dan. 7;8; 11. This

13

application is made by the papists, to save their church from any share in the fulfillment of the prophecy; and in this they have been followed by the mass of opposers to the Advent faith. The following facts show that...

The Little Horn was
Not Antiochus

1. The four kingdoms into which the dominion of Alexander was divided, are symbolized by the four horns of the goat. Now this Antiochus was but one of the twenty-five kings that constituted the Syrian horn. How, then, could he, at the *same time*, be *another* remarkable horn?

2. The ram, according to this vision, became great; the goat waxed very great; but the little horn became exceeding great. How absurd and [11] ludicrous is the following application of this comparison:

Great	Very Great	Exceeding Great
Persia	GRECIA	ANTIOCHUS

How easy and natural is the following:

Great	Very Great	Exceeding Great
Persia	GRECIA	ROME

3. The Medo-Persian Empire is simply called *great*. Verse 4.The Bible informs us that it extended "from India even unto Ethiopia, over an hundred seven and twenty provinces" (Esth. 1:1). This was succeeded by the Grecian power, which is called VERY GREAT (Verse 8). Then comes the power in question which is called EXCEEDING GREAT (Verse 9). Was Antiochus exceeding great when compared with Alexander, the conqueror of the world? Let an item from the

Encyclopedia of Religious Knowledge answer:

"Finding his resources exhausted, he resolved to go into Persia, to levy tributes and collect large sums which he had *agreed to pay to the Romans*"

Surely we need not question which was exceeding great, the Roman power which exacted the tribute, or Antiochus who was *compelled* to pay it.

4. The power in question was "little" at first, but it waxed, or grew, "exceeding great toward the south, and toward the east, and toward the pleasant land". What can this describe but the conquering marches of a mighty power? Rome was almost directly northwest from Jerusalem, and its conquests in Asia and Africa were, of course, toward the east and south; but where were Antiochus' conquests? He came into possession of a kingdom already established, and Sir Isaac Newton says, "He did *not* enlarge it."

5. Out of many reasons that might be added [12] to the above, we named but one. This power was to stand up against the Prince of princes (Verse 25). The Prince of princes is Jesus Christ (Rev. 1:5; 17:14; 19:16). But Antiochus died 164 years before our Lord was born. It is settled, therefore, that another power is the subject of this prophecy. The following facts demonstrate that...

Rome, The Power in Question

1. This power was to come forth from one of the four kingdoms of Alexander's empire. Let us remember that nations are not brought into prophecy, till somehow connected with the people of God. Rome had been inexistence many years before it was noticed in prophecy; and Rome had made Macedon, one of the four horns of the Grecian goat, a part of itself B.C. 168, about ten years before its first connection with the people of God (See 1 Mac. 8). So that Rome could as truly be said to be "out of one of them, " as the *ten horns* of the fourth beast in the seventh chapter, could be said to come *out of that* beast, when they were ten kingdoms set up by the conquerors of Rome.

2. It was to wax exceeding great toward the south, and toward the east, and toward the pleasant land. (Palestine. Ps. 106:24; Zech. 7:14.) This was true of Rome in particular. Witness its conquests in Africa and Asia, and its overthrow of the place and nation of the Jews (John 11:48).

3. It was to cast down of the host and of the stars. This is predicted respecting the dragon (Rev. 12:3, 4). All admit that the dragon was Rome. Who can fail to see their identity?

4. Rome was emphatically a king of fierce [13] countenance, and one that did understand dark sentences. Moses used similar lan-

17

guage when, as all agree, he predicted the Roman power (Deut. 28:49, 50).

5. Rome did destroy wonderfully. Witness its overthrow of all opposing powers.

6. Rome has destroyed more of "the mighty and the holy people, " than all other persecuting powers combined. From fifty to one hundred millions of the church have been slain by it.

7. Rome did stand up against the Prince of princes. The Roman power nailed Jesus Christ to the cross (Acts 4:26, 27; Matt. 27:2; Rev. 12:4).

8. This power is to "be broken without hand." How clear the reference to the stone "cut out without hand" that smote the image (Dan. 2:34). Its destruction then does not take place until the final overthrow of earthly power. These facts are conclusive proof that Rome is the subject of this prophecy. For an extended notice, see *Advent Library*, No. 33.

The field of vision, then, is the empires of Persia, Greece, and Rome.

That part of the vision that now engages our attention is the time—the reckoning of the 2300 days.

The 2300 Days not Explained in Daniel 8

G ABRIEL did explain to Daniel what was meant by the symbols of the beasts and of the horns, but did not in this vision explain to him the 2300 days and the sanctuary. Hence, Daniel tells us at the end of the chapter that he" was astonished at the vision, but none understood it." But there [14] are several facts that will give us some light on this matter.

1. It is a fact that 2300 literal days (not quite seven years) would not cover the duration of a single power in this prophecy, much less extend over them all. Therefore, the days must be symbols, even as the beasts and horns are shown to be symbols.

2. It is a fact that a symbolic or prophetic day is one year (Eze. 4:5, 6; Num. 14:34). Hence, the period is 2300 years

3. The period must begin with "the vision;" consequently it commences in the height of the Medo-Persian power.

But the angel has not yet explained the "manner of time, "or given its date to the prophet. If Gabriel never did explain this subject to Daniel, he is a fallen angel; for he was commanded in plain terms thus to do (Dan. 8:16). But he is not a fallen angel as appears from the fact that some hundred years after this, he was sent to Zacharias and to Mary (Luke 1). Gabriel did explain to Daniel at that time more than he could bear (verse 27), and at a later period, as we shall now show, he did make Daniel understand the vision.

Gabriel Explains in Daniel 9 What He Omitted in Chapter 8

A S we have seen, the charge had been given to Gabriel to make Daniel understand the vision. Verse 16. But in the last verse of the chapter we learn that "none understood"the vision. This must refer particularly to the 2300 days, and to the sanctuary, as the other parts of the vision had been clearly explained.

But in the first verse of chapter 10, he informs [15] us that a thing was revealed to him; "and the thing was true, but *the time appointed was long*; and *he understood the thing*, and had understanding of the vision." Hence, it is evident that between chapters 8 and 10, he must have obtained the desired understanding of the time. In other words, the explanation must be found in chapter 9.

Dan. 9 commences with the earnest, importunate prayer of the prophet, from the reading of which it is evident that he had so far misunderstood the vision of chapter 8, that he concluded that the 2300 days of treading under foot the sanctuary would terminate with the 70 years' desolation of the city and sanctuary predicted by Jeremiah. Compare verses 1 and 2 with verses 16 and 17. The man Gabriel is now sent to undeceive him, and to complete the explanation of the vision. "While I was speaking in prayer, " says Daniel, "even the man Gabriel, whom I had seen in the vision at the beginning [here he cites us back to chapter 8:15, 16], being caused to fly swiftly, touched me about the time of the evening oblation. And he informed me, and talked with me, and said, O Daniel, I am now come forth to give thee skill and *understanding*. At the beginning of thy supplications the commandment came forth, and *I am come to how thee*; for thou art greatly beloved; *therefore understand the matter, and consider the vision*" (Verses 21-23).

Note these facts:

1. In verse 21, Daniel cites us to the vision of chapter 8.
2. In verse 22, Gabriel states that he had come to give Daniel skill and understanding. This being the object of Gabriel's mission, Daniel, who at the close of chapter 8 did not understand the vision, may, ere Gabriel leaves him, fully understand its import
3. As Daniel testifies at the close of chapter 8 that none understood the vision, it is certain that the charge given to Gabriel, "Make this man to understand the vision", still rested upon him. Hence it is that he tells Daniel, "I am now come forth to give thee skill and understanding, " and in verse 23, commands him to "*understand the matter, and to consider the vision.*" This is undeniable proof that Gabriel's mission in chapter 9 was for the purpose of explaining what he omitted in chapter 8. If any ask further evidence, the fact that Gabriel proceeds to explain the very point in question, most fully meets the request. That he does this, we will now show.

Gabriel's Explanation of the Time

SEVENTY weeks are determined upon thy people and upon thy holy city, to finish the transgression, and to make an end of sins, and to make reconciliation for iniquity, and to bring in everlasting righteousness, and to seal up the vision and prophecy, and to anoint the Most Holy. Know therefore and understand, that from the going forth of the commandment to restore and to build Jerusalem unto the Messiah the Prince shall be seven weeks, and threescore and two weeks; the street shall be built again, and the wall, even in troublous times. And after threescore and two weeks shall Messiah be cut off, but not for himself; and the people of the prince that shall come shall destroy the city and the sanctuary; and the end thereof shall be with a flood, and unto the end of the war desolations are determined. And he shall confirm the covenant with many for one week; and in the midst of the week he shall cause the sacrifice and the oblation [17] to cease, and for the overspreading of abominations he shall make it desolate, even until the consummation, and that determined shall be poured upon the desolate" (Dan. 9:24-27).

Determined, in Verse 24 Means Cut Off

S EVENTY weeks are *determined*', literally 'cut off'. The Hebraists all admit that the word determined, in our English version, does signify 'CUT off'. Not one has disputed it" Josiah Litch, *Midnight Cry*, Vol. iv, No. 25.

"Thus Chaldiac and Rabbinical authority, and that of the earliest versions, the Septuagint and Vulgate, give the single signification of 'cutting off' to this verb. Should it be inquired why a tropical sense has been attributed to it, such as 'determining' or 'decreeing, ' it may be answered that the reference of the verse (in which it occurs) to Dan. 8:14, was unobserved. It was therefore supposed that there was no propriety in saying 'seventy weeks are cut off', when there was no other period of which they could have formed a portion. But as the period of 2300 days is first given, and verses 21 and 23, compared with Dan. 8:16, show that the ninth chapter furnishes an explanation of the vision in which Gabriel appeared to Daniel, and of the 'matter'—(the commencement of the 2300 days)—the *literal* (or rather, to speak properly, the only)signification demanded by the subject matter, is that of 'cut off'" —Prof. Whiting, *Midnight Cry*, Vol. iv, No. 17.

"Seventy weeks have been cut off upon thy people and upon thy holy city, to finish the transgression, and to make an end of sin offerings, and to make atonement for iniquity, and to bring in everlasting righteousness, and to seal the vision and prophecy, and to anoint the Most Holy." Dan. 9:24. *Whiting's Translation.*

The facts which are set before us in the above, from Litch and Whiting, should not be forgotten. [18]

1. The word rendered "determined" (verse 24), literally signifies "*cut off*".

2. "*The vision*" which *Gabriel came to explain*, contained the period of 2300 days; and in the explanation he tells us that "seventy weeks have been *cut off*" upon Jerusalem and the Jews. This is a demonstration that the seventy weeks are a part of the 2300 days. Hence the commencement of the seventy weeks is the date of the 2300 days. And the fact that the seventy weeks were fulfilled in 490 years, as all admit, is a demonstration that the 2300 days from which this period of 490 days was cut off, is 2300 years.

The Angel's Date of the Seventy Weeks

W E have seen that the seventy weeks are cut off from the 2300 days. Hence, when the date of the seventy weeks is established, the key to unlock and understand the reckoning of the days is in our hand. The date for the commencement of the weeks is thus given by Gabriel: "Know therefore and understand, that from the going forth of the commandment to restore and to build Jerusalem unto the Messiah the Prince, shall be seven weeks, and threescore and two weeks; the street shall be built again, and the wall, even in troublous times." Dan. 9:25.

We present the following important testimony from the *Advent Herald*. It is a calm, dispassionate vindication of he *original* dates, which establishes them beyond dispute. It was written in the years 1850 and 1851; and, consequently, cannot be supposed to be given with a desire to prove that the days ended in 1844, as the *Herald* is not willing to admit that fact. Therefore it must be regarded as candid and honorable [20] testimony to important facts. That it demolishes every view which has been put forth to readjust the 2300 days, no one, who can appreciate the force of the arguments presented, will fail to perceive. For further testimony the reader is cited to a very valuable work by S. Bliss, entitled, *"Analysis of Sacred Chronology"*. The Herald speaks as follows:

"The Bible gives the data for a complete system of chronology, extending from the creation to the birth of Cyrus, a clearly ascertained date. From this period downward we have the undisputed Canon of Ptolemy, and the undoubted era of Nabonassar, extending below our vulgarera. At the point where inspired chronology leaves us, this Canon of undoubted accuracy commences. And thus the whole arch is spanned. It is by the Canon of Ptolemy that the great prophetical period of seventy weeks is fixed. This Canon places the seventh year of Artaxerxes in the year

B.C. 457; and the accuracy of the Canon is demonstrated by the concurrent agreement of more than twenty eclipses. The seventy weeks date from the going forth of a decree respecting the restoration of Jerusalem. There were no decrees between the seventh and twentieth years of Artaxerxes. Four hundred and ninety years, beginning with the seventh, must commence in B.C. 457, and end in A.D. 34. Commencing in the twentieth, they must commence in B.C. 444, and end in A.D. 47. As no event occurred in A.D. 47 to mark their termination, we cannot reckon from the twentieth; we must, therefore, look to the seventh of Artaxerxes. This date we cannot change from B.C. 457 without first demonstrating the inaccuracy of Ptolemy's Canon. To do this, it would be necessary to show that the large number of eclipses by which its accuracy has been repeatedly demonstrated, have not been correctly computed;and such a result would unsettle every chronological date, and leave the settlement of epochs and the [20] adjustment of eras entirely at the mercy of every dreamer, so that chronology would be of no more value than mere guess work. As the seventy weeks must terminate in A.D. 34, unless the seventh of Artaxerxes is wrongly fixed, and as that cannot be changed without some evidence to that effect, we inquire, What evidence marked that termination? The time when the apostles turned to the Gentiles harmonizes with that better than any other which has been named. And the crucifixion, in A.D. 31, in the midst of the last week, is sustained by a mass of testimony which cannot be easily invalidated."—*Advent Herald*, March 2, 1850.

"The Saviour attended but four Passovers, at the last of which he was crucified. This could not bring the crucifixion later than A.D. 31, as is recorded by Aurelius Cassiodorus, a respectable Roman Senator, about A.D. 514:'In the consulate of Tiberius Caesar Aug. V. and Aelius Sejanus , our Lord Jesus Christ suffered on the eighth of the Calends of April.' In this year, and in this day, says Dr. Hales, agree also the Council of Caesarea, A.D. 196, or 198, the Alexandrian Chronicle, Maximus Monachus, Nicephorus Constantinus, Cedrenus; and in this year, but on different days, concur Eusebius and Epiphanius, followed by Kebler, Bucher, Patinus, and Petavius."—*Advent Herald*, August 24, 1850.

"There are certain chronological points which have been *settled* as *fixed*; and before the seventy weeks can be made to terminate at a later period, those must be unsettled, by being shown to have been fixed on *wrong principles*; and anew date must be assigned for their commencement based on *better principles*. Now that the commencement of the reign of Artaxerxes Longimanus was B.C. 464-3, is demonstrated by the agreement of above twenty eclipses, which have been repeatedly calculated, and have invariably been found to fall in the times specified. Before it can be shown that the commencement of his reign is wrongly fixed, it must first be shown that those eclipses have all been [21] wrongly calculated. This no one has done, or ever will venture to do. Consequently, the commencement of his reign cannot be removed from that point.

"The seventy weeks must date from some decree for the restoration of Jerusalem. Only two events are named in the reign of Artaxerxes for the commencement of those weeks. The one is the decree of the seventh year of his reign, and the other, that of the twentieth. From one of these, those four hundred and ninety years must reckon. As his reign began B.C. 464-3, his seventh year must have been B.C. 458-7; and his twentieth, B.C. 445-4. If the seventy weeks date from the former, they cannot terminate later than A.D. 34; and if from the latter, they cannot have terminated earlier than A.D. 46-7.

"In addition to the above, sixty-nine of the seventy were to extend to the Messiah the Prince. It does not read that they are to terminate when he is called the Prince, or that he is to begin to be the Prince when they terminate. They were to extend to the MESSIAH—the words, the Prince, being added to show *who* was signified by the Messiah. Sixty-nine weeks of years are four hundred and eighty-three years. Beginning these with the seventh of Artaxerxes, they extend to A.D. 26-7; dating from the twentieth, they terminate in A.D. 89-40. Was there anything in either of those years which would make the words, 'unto the Messiah the Prince' appropriate? When Jesus was baptized of John in Jordan, a voice was heard from heaven, acknowledging the Saviour as the Son of God, in whom the Father was well pleased. Consequently, he was 'the messiah the Prince', whose coming had been predicted. With that baptism, the Saviour commenced the work of his public ministry—the Messiah the Prince had then come, as it was predicted he should at the end of the sixty-nine weeks. When he was acknowledged as the Son of God—the Messiah—he went into Galilee preaching the gospel of the kingdom of God, and saying, '*The time is fulfilled*'. The time [22] then fulfilled, must have been some predicted period. There was no predicted period which could then terminate but the sixty-nine or seventy weeks. Did either of these then terminate? We have seen that the former, reckoned from the seventh of Artaxerxes, as it is fixed by astronomical calculations, would end in A.D. 26-7; and A.D. 27 we find is the precise point of time when

28

the Saviour must have been about thirty years of age, when he was baptized of John, and declared the time fulfilled. At the first Passover the Saviour attended, which could not have been later than the spring of his second year, the Jews told him that the temple had been forty-six years in building: reckoning back forty-six years from A.D. 28, they began B.C. 19, which is the precise year when Herod began the work of rebuilding the temple. From the eclipse which marked the death of Herod, before which the Saviour had been born, his birth could not have been later than B.C. 4, which would make him about thirty at the very time of his baptism of John. Such a concurrence of chronological, astronomical, and historical testimony, can only be set aside by testimony still more conclusive.

"Your argument that he was not called a prince till after his crucifixion is of no weight; for the Jews could not have crucified 'the Prince of life, ' as Peter accused them, if he was not the Prince of life till after his crucifixion. Nor is your argument respecting the midst of the week any more to the point. Your criticism has respect only to the English word midst. If you wish to show that it does not mean middle in the present case, you must firsts how that the Hebrew word *chatzi*, which is here translated midst, from the verb *chatzah*, has no such meaning; and that its verb has not 'a *special* signification of dividing into two parts, or to halve'; and that it has not 'a *general sense* of dividing into any number of equal parts', as Hebraists tell us it has. Till you show this, you make no progress whatever toward proving that it does not mean 'middle'. But what was to occur in the *midst* of [23] the week? The 'sacrifice and oblation' were then to cease. Those Jewish ordinances could only cease actually or virtually. They did not actually cease till A.D. 70. They ceased virtually only at the crucifixion; they then ceased to foreshadow the sacrifice then offered. Was that in the midst of the week? 3 ½ years from A.D. 27

bring us to the spring of A.D. 31, where Dr. Hales has demonstrated the crucifixion took place. The week during which the covenant was confirmed was that in the 'midst' of which the sacrifice and oblation virtually ceased. Consequently it could not extend beyond A.D. 34—the latest time to which seventy weeks from the seventh of Artaxerxes Longimanuscould reach." —*Advent Herald*, Feb. 15, 1851.

"Eusebius dates the first half of the Passion Week of years as beginning with our Lord's baptism, and ending with his crucifixion. The same period precisely is recorded by Peter, as including our Lord's *personal* ministry: 'all the time that the Lord Jesus went in and out among us, beginning from the baptism of [or by] John, until the day that he was taken up from us, ' at his ascension, which was only forty-three days after the crucifixion. Acts 1:21, 22. And the remaining half of the Passion Week ended with the martyrdom of Stephen, in the seventh, or last, year of the week. For it is remarkable, that the year after, A.D. 35, began a new era in the church; namely, the conversion of Saul, or Paul, the apostle, by the personal appearance of Christ to him on the road to Damascus, when he received his mission to the Gentiles, after the Jewish Sanhedrin had formally rejected Christ by persecuting his disciples. Acts 9:1-18. And the remainder of the Acts principally records the circumstances of his mission to the Gentiles, and the churches he founded among them."—DR. HALES, as quoted in the *Advent Herald*, March 2, 1850.

The foregoing testimony from the *Herald* establishes the following points:

1. The [24] decree referred to in Dan. 9, from which the 70 weeks are dated, is the decree of the seventh of Artaxerxes, and not that of his twentieth year. Ezra 7. And to this point we deem it duty to append an extract from Prof. Whiting:

    We are informed in Ezra 7:11: 'Now this is the copy of the

letter that the king Artaxerxes gave unto Ezra the priest, the scribe, even a scribe of the words of the commandments of the Lord, and of his statutes to Israel.' The letter then follows, written not in Hebrew, but in Chaldaic [or the Eastern Aramaic], the language then used at Babylon. At the 27th verse, the narrative proceeds in Hebrew. We are thus furnished with the *original* document, by virtue of which Ezra was authorized to 'restore and build Jerusalem;' or, in other words, by which he was clothed with power, not merely to erect walls or houses, but to regulate the affairs of his countrymen in general, to 'set magistrates and judges which may judge all the people beyond the river.' He was commissioned to enforce the observance of the laws of his God, and to punish those who transgressed, with death, banishment, confiscation or imprisonment. See verses 23-27. No grant of powers thus ample, can be found in the case of Nehemiah, or in any other instance after the captivity. That the commission given to Ezra authorized him to proceed in rebuilding the walls of Jerusalem, is evident from the fact that in the twentieth year of Artaxerxes, Nehemiah, who was then in the Persian court, received information that 'the remnant who were left of the captivity, then in the province, were in great affliction and reproach; the wall of Jerusalem was broken down, and the gates thereof burned with fire.' See Nehemiah 1:1-3. The fact is, that Ezra and his associates met with continued opposition from the Samaritans, so that during the whole of the seven weeks, or forty-nine years, from the time that Ezra went up, to [25] the last act of Nehemiah in obliging the Jews to put away their strange wives, the prediction of the prophet was verified—'the street shall be built again, and the wall, even in troublous times.' After Nehemiah reached Jerusalem, he examined the city by night. The result of his examination is thus stated, Nehemiah 2:13: 'And I went out by night, by the gate of the valley, even before the dragon-well, and to the dung-port, and viewed the walls of Jerusalem, which were broken down, and the gates thereof were consumed with fire.' It is evident that 'the walls and gates' which had been destroyed, were the works of Ezra. The impropriety of referring the language of Nehemiah to the destruction of the city by Nebuchadnezzar will be seen at once, if were collect that

> he reduced it to ruins on the capture of Zedekiah, B.C. 588,
> one hundred and forty-four years previous to the time when
> Nehemiah went up to Jerusalem.—*Advent Shield*, No. 1, Ar-
> ticle, Prophetic Chronology, pages 105-6.

That Ezra understood that power was conferred upon himself, and upon the people of Israel, to rebuild the street of Jerusalem and the wall, is certain from his own testimony recorded in chapter 9:9.

2. The second point in the evidence which the *Herald* has adduced, is this: the seventh year of Artaxerxes, from which the decree is dated, is fixed beyond dispute in B.C. 457.

3. The commencement of Christ's ministry in A.D. 27, is clearly established, being just 69 weeks, or 483 prophetic days from the decree in B.C. 457.

4. The crucifixion in the midst of the week is proved to have occurred in the spring of A.D. 31, just three and a half years from the commencement of Christ's ministry.

5. And it further demonstrates that the remaining three and a half years of the seventieth week ended in the autumn of A.D. 34. Here the seventy weeks, which had [26] been cut off upon the Jews, in which they were "to finish the transgression, " close with the Jewish Sanhedrin's act of formally rejecting Christ by persecuting his disciples, and God gives the great apostle to the Gentiles his commission to them. Acts 9. These important dates are clearly and unequivocally established by historical, chronological, and astronomical testimony. Sixty-nine of the 70 weeks from the decree in B.C. 457 ended in A.D. 27, when our Lord was baptized, and began to preach, saying, "The time is fulfilled." Mark 1. Three and a half years from this brings us to the midst of the week in A.D. 31, the period of 70 weeks terminates in the autumn of A.D. 34. Or, to be more definite, the first three and a half years of the seventieth week ended in the first Jewish month (April) in the spring of A.D.

31. The remaining three and a half years would therefore end in the seventh month, autumn of A.D. 34.

Here then we stand at the end of the great period which Gabriel, in explaining the 2300 days to Daniel, tells him was cut off upon Jerusalem and the Jews. Its commencement, intermediate dates, and final termination, are unequivocally established. It remains then to notice this one grand fact: the first 490 years of the 2300 ended in the seventh month, autumn of A.D. 34. This period of 490 years being cut off from the 2300, a period 1810 years remains. This period of 1810 years being added to the seventh month, autumn of A.D. 34, brings us to the seventh month, autumn of 1844. And here, after every effort which has been made to remove the dates, all are [27] compelled to let them stand. For a moment let us recur to the events of 1843 and 1844. Previous to the year 1843, the evidence on the going forth of the decree in B.C. 457 had been clearly and faithfully set forth. And as the period of 457 years before Christ, subtracted from the 2300, would leave but 1843 years after Christ, the end of the 2300 years was confidently expected in 1843. But if the 2300 years began with the commencement of B.C. 457, they would not end till the last day of A.D. 1843, as it would require all of 457, and all of 1843, to make 2300 *full* years.

But at the close of 1843, it was clearly seen that as the crucifixion occurred in the midst of the week, in the spring of A.D. 31, the remainder of the seventieth week, viz.: three and a half years, would end in the autumn of A.D. 34. And as the seventy weeks, or 490 years, ended in the seventh month, autumn of A.D. 34, it is a settled point that the days began, not in the spring, with Ezra's starting from Babylon, but in the autumn, with the commencement of the work at Jerusalem. Ezra 7. And this view, that the days begin with the actual commencement of the work, is much strengthened by the fact that the first seven weeks, or 49 years, are manifestly allotted to the work of restoration in "troublous times." And that period could only begin with the actual commencement of the work. Dan. 9:25.

When it was seen that only 456 years and a fraction had expired before Christ, it was at once understood that 1843 years and a portion of 1844, sufficient to make up a full year when joined to that fraction, was required in order to make 2300 full years. In other words, the 2300 days in full time would expire in the seventh month, 1844. [28] And if we take into the account the fact that the *midst* of the seventieth week was the fourteenth day of the first month, and consequently the *end* of the seventy weeks must have been at a corresponding point in the seventh month, A.D. 34, we perceive at once that the remainder of the 2300 days would end about that point in the seventh month 1844.

It was with this great fact before us, that the 2300 days of Daniel, which reached to the cleansing of the sanctuary, would terminate at that time, and also with the light of the types, that the high priest in "the example and shadow of heavenly things, " on the tenth day of the seventh month, entered within the second veil to cleanse the sanctuary, that we confidently expected the advent of our Redeemer in the seventh month, 1844. The prophecy said, "Then shall the sanctuary be cleansed." The type said that at that season in the year the high priest should pass from the holy place of the earthly tabernacle to the most holy, to cleanse the sanctuary. Lev. 16.

With these facts before us we reasoned as follows:

1. The sanctuary is the earth, or the land of Palestine.
2. The cleansing of the sanctuary is the burning of the earth, or the purification of Palestine, at the coming of Christ.
3. And hence, we concluded that our great High Priest would leave the tabernacle of God in Heaven and descend in flaming fire, on the tenth day of the seventh month, in the autumn of 1844.

It is needless to say that we were painfully disappointed. And, though the man does not live who can overthrow the chronological argument, which terminates the 2300 days at that time, or [29] meet the mighty array of evidence by which it is fortified and sustained, yet multitudes, without stopping to inquire whether our conceptions of the sanctuary and of its cleansing were correct or not, have openly denied the agency of Jehovah in the Advent movement, and have pronounced it the work of man.

An Inexplicable Position

THE position of those Adventists who have attempted to readjust the 2300 days, in order to extend them to some future period in which Palestine should be purified, or the earth be burned, has been, to say the least, extremely embarrassing. In the *Herald* of Dec. 28, 1850, Josiah Litchremarks as follows:

"Chronologically, the *period is at an end*, according to the best light to be obtained on the subject; and where the discrepancy is, I am unable to decide. But of this we shall know more in due time.

'God is his own interpreter, and he will make it plain.'"

But not being able to longer maintain a position in denying the termination of the 2300 years in the past, while at the same time they were setting forth an unanswerable vindication of the original dates for the commencement of the period, the Herald has at last *denied* the *connection* between the 70 weeks and the 2300 days. We write this with deep regret. A correspondent asks the following questions, and the Editor of the *Herald* gives the answers, which are enclosed in brackets:

> "In your 'chronology' the cross is placed A.D. 31. What are the principal objections which bear against its being placed in A.D. 39? [Ans. 1. The absence of any evidence placing it there. 2. The contradiction [30] of the wonderful astronomical, chronological, and historical coincidences which show beyond the shadow of controversy that the seventh of Artaxerxes was in B.C. 457-8, that the birth of Christ was B.C.

4-5, that the thirtieth year of Christ was 483 years from the seventh of Artaxerxes, that the crucifixion was in A.D. 31, and that that was the point of time in the last week, when the sacrifice and oblation should cease.]

"If the seventy weeks of Dan. 9 do not commence in the twentieth of Artaxerxes, how can the 2300 days begin at the same time with them, and yet terminate in the future? [Ans. They cannot.] Must we not henceforth consider that they have different starting points? [Ans. Yes."]—*Advent Herald,* May 22, 1852.

That this is a serious departure from the "original Advent faith, " let the following, which once formed a part of a standing notice in the Advent papers, under the head of "Points of Difference between us and our Opponents, "answer:

"We claim that the ninth of Daniel is an appendix to the eighth, and that the seventy weeks and the 2300 days or years commence together. *Our opponents deny this.*" —*Signs of the Times,* 1843.

The grand principle involved in the interpretation of the 2300 days of Dan. 8:14, is, that the 70 weeks of Dan. 9:24, are the first 490 days of the 2300, of the eighth chapter." —*Advent Shield,* page 49. Article, *The Rise and Progress of Adventism.*

If it is not a serious defection from the original Advent faith to deny "the grand principle involved in the interpretation of the 2300 days of Dan. 8, " and in its place to take the position of "our opponents, " then we greatly err. Hear the opinion of Apollos Hale in 1846:

"The second point to be settled, in explaining the text [Dan. 9:24], is to show what vision it is which the 70 weeks are said to seal. And it should be [31] understood this involves one of the great questions which constitute the main pillars in our system of interpretation, so far as prophetic times are concerned. If the connection between the 70 weeks of Dan. 9, and the 2300 days of Dan. 8, does not exist, the whole system is shaken to its foundation; if it does exist, as we suppose, the system must stand."—*Harmony of Prophetic Chronology*, page 33.

Then the act of those who deny the connection of the 70 weeks and the 2300 days, is of a fearful character. It is a denial of "one of the main pillars in our system of interpretation so far as prophetic times are concerned. If the connection between the 70 weeks of Dan. 9, and the 2300 days of Dan. 8, does not exist, *the whole system is shaken to its foundation.*" And now, reader, will you listen to their reasons for denying the connection between those two periods, which as we have seen is fortified by a mass of direct testimony? They are as follows:

"We have no new light respecting the connection between the 70 weeks and 2300 days. The *only* argument against their connection is, the passing of the time. Why that has passed, is a mystery to us, which we wait to have revealed."—*Advent Herald*, Sept. 7, 1850.

"Before 1843, we became satisfied of the validity of the arguments sustaining their connection and simultaneous commencement. There has nothing transpired to weaken the force of those arguments but the passing of the time we expected for their termination. We now have no other fact to advance against their connection; and, therefore, can only wait for the mystery of the passing of time to be explained. But of the commencement and termination of the 70 weeks, we are satisfied that they cannot be removed from the position which Protestants have always assigned them."—*Advent Herald*, Feb. 22, 1851. [32]

In its appropriate place, we offered conclusive testimony to prove the connection of the 70 weeks and 2300 days. And it is submitted to the reader's judgment whether the reasons offered to disprove that connection are entitled to any weight or not. It will be seen that they grow out of the assumed correctness of the view that the earth, or the land of Canaan, is the sanctuary, and that the cleansing of the sanctuary is the burning of the earth, or the purification of Palestine at the coming of Christ. Before the reader adopts the conclusion that the 70 weeks, which Gabriel says were "cut off, " are no part of the great period contained in the vision which he was explaining to Daniel, we request him to follow us in the inquiry: What is the sanctuary, and how is it to be cleansed? This we shall presently follow out, and in doing it, we may discover the cause of our disappointment.

THERE ARE TWO "DESOLATIONS" IN DAN. 8—This fact is made so plain by Josiah Litch that we present his words:

"'The daily *sacrifice*' is the present reading of the English text. But no such thing as *sacrifice* is found in the original. This is acknowledged on all hands. It is a gloss or construction put on it by the translators. The true reading is, 'the daily and the transgression of desolation, ' daily and transgression being connected together by 'and;' the *daily desolation* and the *transgression of desolation*. They are two desolating powers, which were to desolate the sanctuary and the host."—*Prophetic Expositions*, Vol. i, page 127.

It is plain that the sanctuary and the host were to be trodden under foot by the daily and the transgression of desolation. The careful reading of verse 13 settles this point. And this fact establishes [33] another, viz.: that these two desolations are the *two grand forms* under which Satan has attempted to overthrow the worship and the cause of Jehovah. Mr. Miller's remarks on the meaning of these two terms, and the course pursued by himself in ascertaining that meaning, is presented under the following head:...

The Two Desolations are Paganism and Papacy

I read on, and could find no other case in which it [the daily] was found, but in Daniel. I then [by the aid of a concordance] took those words which stood in connection with it, '*take way*;' he shall *take away*, 'the daily; ' from the time the daily shall be *taken away*', etc. I read on, and thought I should find no light on the text; finally, I came to 2 Thess. 2:7, 8. 'For the mystery of iniquity doth already work; only he who now letteth will let, until he be *taken out of the way*, and then shall that wicked be revealed, ' etc. And when I had come to that text, oh! how clear and glorious the truth appeared! There it is! That is' the daily!' Well now, what does Paul mean by 'he who now letteth, ' or hindereth? By 'the man of sin, ' and the 'wicked, ' popery is meant. Well, what is it which hinders popery from being revealed? Why, it is paganism; well, then, 'the daily' must mean paganism."—*Second Advent Manual*, page 66.

It needs no argument to prove that the two grand forms of opposition, by which Satan has desolated the church and trod under foot the sanctuary of the living God, are none other than paganism and popery. It is also a clear point that the change from one of these desolations to the other did occur under the Roman power. Paganism, from the days of the kings of Assyria, down to the period when it became so far modified that it took the [34] name of popery, had been

40

the daily (or, as Prof. Whiting renders it, "the continual")desolation, by which Satan had stood up against the cause of Jehovah. And, indeed, in its priests, its altars and its sacrifices, it bore resemblance to the Levitical form of Jehovah's worship. When the Christian form of worship took the place of the Levitical, a *change* in Satan's form of opposition, and counterfeit worship, became necessary, if he would successfully oppose the worship of the great God. And it is in the light of these facts that we are able to understand our Lord's reference to the abomination of desolation in Matt. 24:15. It is evident that he there cites Dan. 9:26, 27. Now, although we do not understand that paganism in the year 70 had given place to popery, we do understand that that same power which then appeared, modified somewhat in name and form, was the very power that should, as the abomination of desolation, wear out the saints of the Most High.

The language of Paul is to the point: "For the mystery of iniquity [popery] *doth already work*; only he who now letteth will let, until he be taken out of the way. And then shall that Wicked be revealed, whom the Lord shall consume with the Spirit of his mouth, and shall destroy with the brightness of his coming." 2 Thess. 2:7, 8. That Paul refers to paganism and popery, none question. And here is direct proof that popery, the abomination of desolation, had in Paul's day already begun to work. Nor was it a very great change of character when Satan transformed his counterfeit worship from paganism to popery. The same temples, altars, incense, priests and worshipers were ready, with little change, to serve as the appendages of the papal abomination. The [35] statute of Jupiter readily changed to that of Peter, the prince of the apostles; and the Pantheon, which had been the temple of all the gods, without difficulty became the sanctuary of all the saints. Thus the same abomination that desolated Jerusalem, in a degree changed and modified, became the wonderful desolater of the saints and martyrs

41

of Jesus. And in its so-called temple of God, it set at naught and trod under foot the true temple of Jehovah, and he who is its minister, Jesus Christ. The change from paganism to popery is clearly shown in John's view of the transfer of power from the dragon of Rev. 12, to the beast of Rev. 13. And that they are essentially the same thing, is evident from the fact that both the dragon and the beast are represented with *the* seven heads; thus showing that, in a certain sense, either may be understood to cover the whole time. And in the same sense we understand that either abomination covers all the period. Christ's reference to the abomination of desolation (Matt. 24:15; Luke 21:20) is an absolute demonstration that Rome is the little horn of Dan. 8:9-12. Having shown that there are two desolations, by which the sanctuary and the host are trodden down, we now notice the fact that there are...

Two Opposing Sanctuaries of Daniel 8

TO the careful reader this fact will at once appear. They are as follows: First, the sanctuary of the daily desolation. Verse 11; 11:31. Second, the sanctuary which the daily and the transgression of desolation were to tread under foot. Verses 13, 14. The one is the sanctuary of Satan; the other is the sanctuary of the Lord of hosts. The one is the dwelling place of "all the gods;" the other is the habitation of the only living and true God. If it be said that a sanctuary is never connected with heathen and idolatrous worship, we cite the direct testimony of the Bible. Heathen Moab had a sanctuary. And that sanctuary was a place of prayer and worship for that heathen nation. Isa 16:12. The chapel erected by the king of Israel at Bethel, as a rival to the temple of God at Jerusalem (1 Kings 12:27, 31-33) was called his sanctuary. Amos 7:13, margin. And the places in which idolatrous Israel (the ten tribes)worshiped, are called sanctuaries. Amos 7:9. The same is true of idolatrous Tyre. Eze. 28:18. Attention is called to the following from Apollos Hale:

> "What can be meant by the 'sanctuary' of paganism? Paganism, and error of every kind, have their sanctuaries as well as truth. These are the temples or asylums consecrated to their service. Some particular and renowned temple of paganism may, then, be supposed to be here spoken of. Which of its numerous distinguished temples may it be? One of the most

43

magnificent specimens of classic architecture is called the Pantheon. The name signifies *'the temple or asylum of all the gods.'* The 'place' of its location is Rome. The idols of the nations conquered by the Romans were sacredly deposited in some niche or apartment of this temple, and in many cases became objects of worship by the Romans themselves. Could we find a temple of paganism that was more strikingly *'his sanctuary'?* Was Rome, the city or place of the Pantheon, 'cast down' by the authority of the State? Read the following well-known and remarkable facts in history: 'The death of the last rival of Constantine had sealed the peace of the empire. Rome was once more the undisputed queen of nations. But, in the hour of elevation and splendor, she had been raised to the edge of a precipice. Her [37] next step was to be downward and *irrecoverable.* The change of the government transcontinental still perplexes the historian. Constantine abandoned Rome, the great citadel and throne of the Caesars, for an obscure corner of Thrace, and expended the remainder of his vigorous and ambitious life in the doublet oil of raising a colony into the capital of his empire, *and degrading the capital into the feeble honors and humiliated strength of a colony'"—Second Advent Manual,* page 68.

And not only did Satan possess himself of a rival to the sanctuary of Jehovah in the period of pagan worship, but, throughout the Christian dispensation, has that arch fiend possessed a rival temple of God. 2 Thess. 2:4. Thus much for the rival sanctuary of Satan. The sanctuary of God remains to be noticed at length. Connected with these two sanctuaries, ...

There are two Hosts in Daniel 8:9-13

THE one is the host that was given to the little horn against the daily, when it had filled its measure of transgression; and by the aid of this host, the little horn was able to cast down the truth. Verse 12. This host is mentioned in Dan. 11:31. By this host, the sanctuary of the daily desolation, and its services, were transferred to the transgression, or abomination of desolation. This host is the forces of Satan, and it is intimately associated with his sanctuary. The other host is "the host of heaven."Verse 10. Michael is the Prince of this host. Dan. 10:21. Against the Prince of this host, the little horn stands up. Verses 11, 25. (Prof. Whiting remarks that in the original, "Prince of the host" occurs in Josh. 5:14) None dispute that the host, of whom Michael (Christ) is Prince, is the church of the [38] living God. Dan. 12:1.

This host, the true church, is fitly represented by a green olive tree. Jer. 11:15-17. And when some of the branches (members of the Jewish church) were broken off through unbelief, others were grafted in from the Gentiles, and thus the host continues to exist. Rom. 11:17-20. This host, or church, is the worshipers of God, and is intimately connected with his sanctuary. That sanctuary we are now prepared to consider.

What is the
Sanctuary of God?

B EFORE answering this question, we present the definition of the word sanctuary: "A holy place."—Walker. "A sacred place."—Webster. "A holy or sanctified place a dwelling-place of the Most High."—Cruden. A dwelling-place for God. Ex. 25:8. Thus much for the meaning of the word. We now inquire respecting its application.

Is The Earth The Sanctuary? To this question we answer emphatically: *It is not*. And if we are requested to *prove a negative,* we offer the following reasons:

1. The word sanctuary is used 145 times in the Bible, and it is not in a single instance applied to the earth. Hence there is no authority for this view, except that of man.

2. Every one knows that the earth is neither a dwelling-place of God, nor yet a holy, or sacred place. Those, therefore, who affirm that it is the sanctuary of God, should know better than to make such a statement.

3. In almost every instance in which the word sanctuary occurs in the Bible (and the exceptions nearly all refer to Satan's rival sanctuary) it refers directly to another definite object which God calls his sanctuary. Hence, those who [39] teach that the earth is the sanctuary of the Lord of hosts, contradict his positive testimony a hundred times repeated. For the benefit oft hose who think that

the earth will become the sanctuary after it has been cleansed by fire, we add that God does not even then call it his sanctuary, but simply "the *place*"of its location. Isa. 60:13; Eze. 37:26-28; Rev. 21:1-3. The earth, then, is not the sanctuary, but merely the *place* where it will be located hereafter.

Is THE CHURCH THE SANCTUARY?—We answer: It is not. The following reasons in support of this answer are to the point:

1. The Bible never calls the church the sanctuary.

2. In a great number of texts, God has called another object his sanctuary, and has uniformly associated the church with that object, as the worshipers; and that sanctuary itself, as the place of that worship, or toward which their prayer was directed. Ps. 20:2; 28:2, margin;29:2, margin; 63:2; 68:24; 73:17; 134:2; 150:1; 5:7.

3. The following *inference* is *all* that we have ever seen urged in favor of this view. God has many times called the tabernacle or temple, which are the patterns of the true, his sanctuary. And because that the church is spiritually called the temple of God, some have supposed that they were at liberty to call the church the sanctuary.

4. But there is one text that some may urge. It is this: "When Israel went out of Egypt, the house of Jacob from a people of strange language; Judah was his sanctuary, and Israel his dominion." Ps. 114:1, 2. But, at most, this would only prove that one of the twelve tribes was the sanctuary, and that the whole church was not. But if the fact be remembered, that God chose Jerusalem [40] (2 Chron. 6:6), which was in Judah (Josh. 15:63; Judges 1:8; Zech. 1:12; Ezra 1:3), as the place of his sanctuary (1 Chron. 28:9, 10; 2 Chron. 3:1), we think the following from another psalm willfully explain the connection between Judah and the sanctuary of God, and show that Judah was the tribe with which God designed to locate his habitation: "But chose the tribe

47

of Judah, the Mount Zion which he loved. And he built his sanctuary like high palaces [see 1 Chron. 29:1], like the earth which he hath established forever." Ps. 78:68, 69.

5. But if a single text could be adduced to prove that the church is called a sanctuary, the following plain fact would prove beyond controversy that it is not the sanctuary of Dan. 8:13, 14. The church is represented in Dan. 8:13, by the word "host." This none will deny. "To give *both* the sanctuary and the host to be trodden under foot." Then the church and the sanctuary are two things. The church is the host or worshipers; the sanctuary is the place of that worship, or the place toward which it is directed.

IS THE LAND OF CANAAN THE SANCTUARY?—Of the 145 times in which the word sanctuary occurs in the Bible, only two or three texts have been urged, with any degree of confidence, as referring to the land of Canaan. Yet, strangely enough, men have claimed that the supposed meaning of these two or three texts ought to determine the signification of the word in Dan. 8:13, 14, against the plain testimony of more than a hundred texts! For none can deny that in almost every instance in which the word does occur, it refers directly to the typical tabernacle, or else to the true, of which [42] that was but the figure or pattern. But we now inquire whether the two or three texts in question do actually apply the word sanctuary to the land of Canaan. They read as follows: "Thou shalt bring them in, and plant them in the mountain of thine inheritance, in the place, O Lord, which thou hast made for thee to dwell in; in the sanctuary, O Lord, which thy hands have established." Ex.15:17. "And he led them on safely, so that they feared not;but the sea overwhelmed their enemies. And he brought them to the border of his sanctuary, even to this mountain, which his right hand had purchased." "And he built his sanctuary like high palaces, like the earth which he hath established forever." Ps. 78:53, 54, 69.

The first of these texts, it will be noticed, is taken from the song of Moses, after the passage of the Red Sea. It is a prediction of what God would do for Israel. The second text was written about five hundred years after the song of Moses. What Moses utters as a *prediction*, the psalmist records as a *matter of history*. Hence the psalm is an *inspired commentary* on the song of Moses. If the first text be read without the other, the idea might be gathered that the mountain was the sanctuary, though it does not directly state this. Even as one might get the idea that the tribe of Judah was Mount Zion, were they to read only the expression, "but chose the tribe of Judah, the Mount Zion which he loved" (Ps. 78:68), and omit those texts which inform us that Mount Zion was the city of David, a part of Jerusalem (2 Sam. 5:6, 7), and was *located in Judah*, as one of its cities. Ezra 1:3; Ps. 69:35.

But if the second text be read in connection with the first, it destroys the possibility of such [43] an inference. The psalmist states that the mountain of the inheritance was the border of the sanctuary. And that God, *after* driving out the heathen before his people, proceeded to *build his sanctuary* like high palaces. See 1 Chron. 29:1.

1. The land of Canaan was the mountain of the inheritance. Ex. 15:17.

2. That mountain of the *border* of the sanctuary. Ps. 78:54.

3. In that border God *built* his sanctuary. Ps. 78:69.

4. In that sanctuary God dwelt. Ps. 74:7; Ex. 25:8.

5. In that border the people dwelt. Ps. 78:54, 55. These facts demonstrate that the same Spirit moved both those "holy men of old." These texts perfectly harmonize, not only with each other, but with the entire testimony of the Bible, respecting the sanctuary. If the reader still persists in confounding the sanctuary with its border, the land of Canaan, we request him to listen while a king of Judah points out the distinction:

> "Art not thou our God, who didst drive out the inhabitants of *this land* before thy people Israel, and gavest it to the seed of Abraham thy friend forever? And they dwelt *therein*, and have *built* thee a *sanctuary therein* for thy name, saying, If, when evil cometh upon us, as the sword, judgment, or pestilence, or famine, we stand before this *house*, and in thy presence (for thy name is in this *house*), and cry unto thee in our affliction, then thou wilt hear and help." 2 Chron. 20:7-9.

This language is a perfect parallel to that of Ps. 78:54, 55, 69. In the clearest manner it points out the distinction between the land of Canaan and the sanctuary which was built therein; and it does clearly teach that that sanctuary was the house erected as the habitation of God. [43]

But there is another text by which some attempt to prove that Canaan is the sanctuary. "The people of thy holiness have possessed it but a little while: our adversaries have trodden down thy sanctuary." Isa. 63:18. No one offers this as direct testimony. As it is only an inference, a few words are all that is needed.

1. When the people of God's holiness were driven out of the land of Canaan (as here predicted by the prophet, who uses the past tense for the future), not only were they dispossessed of their inheritance, but the sanctuary of God, built in that land, was laid in ruins. This is plainly stated in 2 Chron. 36:17-20.

2. The next chapter testifies that the prophet had a view of the destruction of God's sanctuary, as stated in the text quoted from 2 Chronicles. This explains thew hole matter. Isa. 64:10, 11; Ps. 74:3, 7; 79:1.

A fourth text may occur to some minds as conclusive proof that Canaan is the sanctuary. We present it, as it is the only remaining one that has ever been urged in support of this view. "The glory of Lebanon shall come unto thee, the fir tree, the pine tree, and the box together, to beautify the place of my sanctuary; and I will make the place of my feet glorious." Isa. 60:13. This text needs little comment. The place of God's sanctuary, we fully admit, is the land of Canaan, or the new earth, for Isaiah refers to the glorified state. And as God has promised to set his sanctuary in that place (Eze. 37:25-28), the meaning of the text is perfectly plain. But if any still assert that the place of the sanctuary is the sanctuary itself, let them notice that the same text calls the same "place" the place of the Lord's feet; and hence the same principle would [44] make the land of Canaan the feet of the Lord! The view that Canaan is the sanctuary is too absurd to need further notice. And even were it a sanctuary, it would not even then be *the* sanctuary of Daniel; for the prophet had his eye upon the habitation of God. Dan. 9. Canaan was only the place of God's sanctuary or habitation.

We have found that the earth is not the sanctuary, but simply the territory where it will finally be located; that the church is not the sanctuary, but simply the worshipers connected with the sanctuary; and that the land of Canaan is not the sanctuary, but that it is the place where the typical sanctuary was located. Now we inquire for the sanctuary itself.

Bible View of
the Sanctuary

THE sanctuary of the Bible is the habitation of God. It includes, first, the tabernacle pitched by man, which was the pattern of the true; and second, the true tabernacle which the Lord pitched and not man. The tabernacle erected by man, as the pattern of the true, embraced, first, the tabernacle of Moses, second, the temple of Solomon, and, third, the temple of Zerubbabel. The true tabernacle of God is the great original of which Moses, Solomon, and Zerubbabel, erected "figures, " "patterns, " or "images." We trace the pattern of the true from the time it was erected by Moses, until it was merged into the larger and more glorious pattern which Solomon caused to be established. We trace this building down to the period when it was overthrown by Nebuchadnezzar, and suffered to remain in ruins through the Babylonish captivity. And from the time that Zerubbabel rebuilt the sanctuary, we trace the [45] history of the pattern until we reach the true tabernacle, the great sanctuary of Jehovah. We trace the history of the tabernacle from the time that our Lord entered it to minister in "the holy places" for us, forward to the time when it shall be located on the New Earth, when the tabernacle and sanctuary of God shall be with his people forever. We are compassed about with a great cloud of witnesses. To the law and to the testimony. We gather our first instruction respecting the sanctuary from the book of

Exodus. In chapter 24, we learn that Moses went up into the cloud that enshrouded the God of Israel, upon the Mount Sinai, and that he was there forty days. It was during this period that the building of the sanctuary was explained to Moses, and the pattern of it shown to him in that mount. Heb. 8:5.

The next chapter commences with

THE COMMANDMENT TO ERECT THE SANCTUARY—"And the Lord spake unto Moses, saying, Speak unto the children of Israel, that they bring me an offering; of every man that giveth it willingly with his heart ye shall take my offering. And this is the offering which ye shall take of them; gold, and silver, and brass, and blue, and purple, and scarlet, and fine linen, and goats' hair, and rams' skins dyed red, and badgers' skins, and shittim wood, oil for the light, spices for anointing oil, and for sweet incense, onyx stones, and stones to be set in the ephod, and in the breastplate. And let them make me a sanctuary; that I may dwell among them. According to all that I show thee, after the pattern of the tabernacle, and the pattern of all the instruments thereof, even so shall ye make it." Ex. 25:1-9.

We have here learned several important facts: [46]

1. The sanctuary was the habitation of God. It was erected for this express purpose, that God might dwell among his people. And Moses had his eye upon this habitation, or sanctuary, in that very chapter in which he is supposed, by some, to teach that the land of Canaan is the sanctuary."He is my God, " says Moses, "and I will prepare him an habitation." Chap. 15:2. It is plain that, even then, Moses understood the difference between the habitation of Jehovah and the place of its location.

2. The sanctuary, which God commanded Moses to erect, was the tabernacle. The tabernacle of witness was the sanctuary of God.

3. Moses was solemnly enjoined to make the sanctuary, and all

its vessels, according to the pattern shown to him in that place. Hence, we are now to have a model of the habitation of God set before us.

THE PLAN OF THE SANCTUARY.—Its walls on the north, the west, and the south sides, were formed of upright boards, set in sockets of silver. These boards were ten cubits in length, by one cubit and a half in breadth. And as there were twenty of them on each of the two sides, we learn that it was thirty cubits in length and ten in height. In the same manner, we ascertain that it was about ten cubits in width. The sockets in which the boards were set, are termed, "the sockets of the *sanctuary*" Chap. 38:27. Five bars running the length of the sides, and passing through rings in the boards, joined them all together. And the whole was overlaid with gold. The sanctuary was covered with four different coverings. The east end was closed by a veil, or hanging, called the door of the tent or tabernacle. A second veil divided the tabernacle into two parts [47] called the holy place, and the holiest of all. Chap. 26:1-29, 31-37; 36:8-38; Lev. 16:2; Heb. 9:3.

THE VESSELS OF THE SANCTUARY.—These were all made after the pattern which the Lord showed to Moses. Ex. 25:9, 40. They were as follows:

1. The ark. This was a small chest about four feet six inches in length, and about two feet six inches in width and height, over-laid with pure gold, within and without. This was made for the express purpose of containing God's testament, the ten command-ments. Chap. 25:10-16, 21; 31:8; 32:15, 16; 37:1-5; Deut. 10:1-5; 1 Kings 8:9; 2 Chron. 5:10; Heb. 9:4.

2. The mercy seat. This was the top of the ark. On either end of it stood a cherub. The cherubim and the mercy seat being one solid work of beaten gold. Ex. 25:17-22; 37:6-9; 26:34; Heb. 9:4, 5.

3. The altar of incense. This was overlaid with gold, and was about

three and a half feet in height, and nearly two feet square. It was for the purpose of burning incense before God. Ex. 30:1-10; 37:25-28; Luke 1:9-11.

4. The golden censer. This was used to burn incense before the Lord, particularly in the holiest. Lev. 10:1; 16:12; Heb. 9:4.

5. The candlestick, with its seven lamps, was one solid work of beaten gold, about the weight of a talent. It was made after the express pattern shown to Moses. Ex. 25:31-40;37:17-24; Num. 8:4.

6. The table of show-bread. This was about three and a half feet in length, two and a half in height, and two in width. It was overlaid with pure gold, and on it, show-bread was always kept before the Lord. Ex. 25:23-30; 37:10-16; Heb. 9:2.

7. The [48] altar of burnt offering. This was about nine feet square, and nearly five and a half feet in height. It was overlaid with brass, and was, as its name implies, used for the purpose of offering up sacrifices to God. Ex. 27:1-8; 37:1-7.

8. The laver. This was made of brass, and contained water for the use of the priests. Chap. 30:18-21; 38:8. The court of the tabernacle was one hundred cubits in length, by fifty in breadth, and five cubits, or about nine feet, in height. Chap. 27:9-19; 38:8-20.

God called those who were to execute this work by name, and filled them with the spirit of wisdom. Chap. 31:1-11;35:30-35. They knew "how to make all manner of work for the service of the sanctuary." Chap. 36:1. They received the offering of the children of Israel for "the service of the sanctuary." Verse 3. They came from the "work of the sanctuary" (verse 4), and testified that more was offered than could be used. And Moses commanded that none should "make any more work for the offering of the sanctuary."Verse 6. The construction of every part of the sanctuary is minutely described in chaps. 36-39. Everything was then submitted to Moses for inspection, and he pronounced the work such as God commanded, viz.: a true pattern. Chap. 39:33-43. God then commanded Moses to set up the sanctuary, and to place everything in order. Chap. 40:1-16.

MOSES ERECTS THE SANCTUARY.—And Moses reared up the tabernacle, and set up its boards in the sockets of silver, and united them together by the bars, and spread over the whole, the covering of the tabernacle. He then placed the testimony in the ark, and set the mercy seat upon it, and [49]carried the ark into the tabernacle. Chap. 40:17-21. He then hung up the veil in front of the ark, and thus divided between the holy places. Verse 21; 26:33; Heb. 9:3. He placed the table without the veil, on the north side of the holy place, and set the bread in order upon it. Verses 22, 23. He then placed the candlestick on the south side of the holy place, and lighted its lamps before the Lord. Verses 24, 25. He placed the golden altar before the veil, in the holy place, and burned sweet incense upon it. Verses 26, 27. He set up the hanging for the door of the sanctuary, and he placed the altar of burnt offering at the door, and set the laver between the tabernacle and this altar, and around the whole, he set up the court of the tabernacle. Verses 28-33. The sanctuary erected for the habitation of Jehovah (Ex. 15:2; 25:8) is now ready to receive the King Eternal.

GOD TAKES POSSESSION OF THE SANCTUARY.—"Then the cloud covered the tent of the congregation, and the glory of the Lord filled the tabernacle. And Moses was not able to enter into the tent of the congregation, because the cloud abode thereon, and the glory of the Lord filled the tabernacle."Verses 34, 35. We now have found the habitation, or sanctuary, of the Lord. In the book of Exodus, Moses calls this building the sanctuary at least eleven times. But do you ask for the words of the New Testament on the point? Then listen.

PAUL'S VIEW OF THE SANCTUARY OF THE FIRST COVENANT.—"Then verily the first covenant had also ordinances

56

of divine service, and a worldly sanctuary. For there was a tabernacle made; the first, wherein was the candlestick, and the [50] table, and the show-bread; which is called the sanctuary. And after the second veil, the tabernacle which is called the Holiest of all; which had the golden censer, and the ark of the covenant overlaid round about with gold, wherein was the golden pot that had manna, and Aaron's rod that budded, and the tables of the covenant; and over it the cherubim of glory shadowing the mercy seat." Heb. 9:1-5; 13:11. It is settled, therefore, that we have the right view of this subject thus far, and that the tabernacle of God, and not the land of Canaan, was the sanctuary.

THE WORLDLY SANCTUARY WAS THE PATTERN OF THE TRUE.—"After the pattern of the tabernacle, and the pattern of all the instruments thereof, even so shall ye make it." "And look that thou make them after their pattern, which was showed thee in the mount." Ex. 25:9, 40. "And thou shalt rear up the tabernacle according to the fashion thereof which was showed thee in the mount." Chap. 26:30. "As it was showed thee in the mount so shall they make it." Chap. 27:8."According unto the pattern which the Lord had showed Moses, so he made the candlestick." Num. 8:4. "Our fathers had the tabernacle of witness in the wilderness, as he had appointed, speaking unto Moses, that he should make it according to the fashion that he had seen." Acts 7:44. "Who serve unto the *example and shadow of heavenly things,* as Moses was admonished of God when he was about to make the tabernacle; for, see, saith he, that thou make all things according to the pattern showed to thee in the mount." Heb. 8:5. "It was therefore necessary that *the patterns of things in the heavens* should be purified with these; but the [51] heavenly things themselves with better sacrifices than these. For Christ is not entered into the holy places made with hands, which are the *figures of the true.*" Heb. 9:23, 24. From these texts we learn two important facts.

1. We are many times certified that the tabernacle of witness was made according to the pattern which God showed to Moses.
2. That that pattern was a representation of the heavenly sanctuary itself. Heb. 8:2.

We trace the history of the sanctuary in the book of Leviticus. Every instance in which the word occurs, it is admitted, refers to the tabernacle of the Lord. The blood of sin offering was sprinkled "before the veil of the sanctuary." Lev. 4:6. For offering strange fire before the Lord in his tabernacle, two of the sons of Aaron were slain. They were then carried "from before the sanctuary."Lev. 10:4. The unclean were not to "come into the sanctuary, " or tabernacle. Lev. 12:4, 6. "The holy sanctuary" was to be cleansed. Lev. 16:16, 33. "Ye shall keep my Sabbaths, and reverence my sanctuary; I am the Lord." Lev. 19:30; 26:2. Those who worshiped Moloch, defiled the Lord's sanctuary. Lev. 20:3. "Sanctuaries, "used for the two holy places. Lev. 21:23; 26:31. See also Jer. 51:51. God commanded that the high priest should not"go out of the sanctuary, nor profane the sanctuary of his God, " to mourn for the dead. Lev. 21:12.

God placed his tabernacle in the charge of the tribe of Levi, who pitched around it. Num. 1:50-53. Under the standard of Judah on the east, of Reuben on the south, of Ephraim on the west, and of Dan on the north, the tribes of Israel were [52] to pitch around the tabernacle in four great bodies, during their sojourn in the wilderness. Num. 2. God then divided the tribe of Levi according to his three sons, Gershon, Kohath, and Merari. These three divisions were to pitch severally on the west, south, and north sides of the tabernacle. Num. 3. The Kohathites were to keep "the charge of the sanctuary, " and also of "the vessels of the sanctuary." Verses 28, 31. And Eleazar, the priest, was to have the oversight of those who thus kept "the charge of the sanctuary." Verse 32. But on the east side of the tabernacle, Moses,

Aaron, and his sons, were to encamp, and keep "the charge of the sanctuary." Verse 38.

When the camp was to set forward, the priests were to take down the tabernacle (Num. 4), and cover the sacred vessels, and "all the instruments of ministry wherewith they minister in the sanctuary" (verse 12); and when they had made an end of covering the sanctuary, and all the vessels of the sanctuary, the sons of Kohath were to bear it. Verse 15. And God commanded that Eleazar should have "the oversight of all the tabernacle, and of all that therein is, in the sanctuary." Verse 16. "The service of the sanctuary, " belonging unto the Kohathites, was to bear it upon their shoulders. Num. 7:9. The Levites were given to Aaron to do the service of the tabernacle, that there be no plague "when the children of Israel come nigh unto the sanctuary." Num. 8:19. "The Kohathites set forward bearing the sanctuary." Num. 10:21.

The priests were to "bear the iniquity of the sanctuary."Num. 18:1. The Levites were not to "come nigh the vessels of the sanctuary." Verse 3. And the priests should "keep the [53] charge of the sanctuary." Verse 5. The man that neglected purification, "defiled the sanctuary of the Lord." Num. 19:20. "The shekel of the sanctuary, " or tabernacle, was the standard in Israel. The word sanctuary, meaning the habitation of God, occurs in this connection twenty-five times. Ex. 30:13, 24; 38:24, 25, 26; Lev. 5:15;27:3, 25; Num. 3:47, 50; 7:13, 19, 25, 31, 37, 43, 49, 55, 61, 67, 73, 79, 85, 86; 18:16.

The word sanctuary does not occur in the book of Deuteronomy. One chapter refers to it as "the tabernacle of the congregation." 31:14, 15. We have traced the history of the sanctuary, from the time that it was erected, through the period of Israel's sojourn in the wilderness. From Acts 7:45, we learn that the tribes of Israel carried it with them into the promised land. In the book of Joshua it is called the house of God, or tabernacle; and we learn that it was set up at Shiloh.

Josh. 9:23; 18:1; 19:51; Jer. 7:12. It is called the Lord's tabernacle. Josh. 22:19. It is called "the sanctuary of the Lord." Josh. 24:26. In the book of Judges it is simply called "the house of God, "located at Shiloh. Judges 18:31; 20:18, 26, 31; 21:2. In 1 Samuel it is termed the house of the Lord. Chap. 1:7, 24; 3:15. In chapters 1:9; 3:3, it is called the temple of the Lord. In chapter 2:32, God calls it "my habitation, " or tabernacle, margin. It still abode in Shiloh. Chap. 4:4.

GOD FORSAKES THE SANCTUARY.—For the gross wickedness of the priests and people (1 Sam. 2), God forsook his habitation, and gave his glory (the ark of his testament)into the hands of the [54] enemy, the Philistines. Ps. 78:60-62;Jer. 7:12-14; 1 Sam. 4. It does not appear that after the ark of God was taken from the tabernacle at Shiloh, and God there forsook his habitation, that his glory, or the ark of his covenant, ever returned to that building. The other sacred vessels remained with the tabernacle which, in the days of Saul, seems to have been located at Nob (1 Sam. 21;Matt. 12:3, 4; Mark 2:26); and in the days of David, at Gibeon. 1 Chron. 16:39; 21:29, 30; 1 Kings 3:4; 2 Chron. 1:3. And here we leave it for the present to follow the ark.

The ark was taken by the Philistines, and kept in their land seven months. In which time they were smitten with sore plagues, and Dagon, their god, twice fell before it. They then returned it to Israel to Beth-shemesh. At this place 50, 000 of Israel were smitten for looking into the ark. 1 Sam. 4; 5; 6. From thence it was removed to Kirjath•jearim to the house of Abinadab, where it abode twenty years. 1 Sam. 7:1, 2. In this period it is said that all Israel "lamented after the Lord." From this place it was removed to the house of Obed-edom, where it abode three months. 2 Sam. 6:1-11; 1 Chron. 13. From this place David removed it to his own city, Jerusalem, and placed it in a tabernacle which he had pitched. 2 Sam. 6:12-17; 1 Chron. 15; 16:1.

It was at this time, when the Lord had given David rest from all his enemies, and he dwelt securely in his own house, that the habitation of his God came before his mind.

DAVID DESIRES TO BUILD A GLORIOUS SANCTUARY.— The situation of God's house came into the mind of David, and he "desired to find a [55] tabernacle for the God of Jacob." Acts 7:46; Ps. 132:1-5. He set this matter before Nathan the prophet, who said to him, "Do all that is in thy heart, for God is with thee." But that night God charged Nathan to say to David, "Thus saith the Lord, thou shalt not build me a house to dwell in." 1 Chron. 17:1-4; 2 Sam. 7:1-5. This was because David had been a man of war, and had shed blood abundantly. But God promised that Solomon, his son, should build the house. 1 Chron. 22:7-10. Then David proceeded to make great preparation for the building. Chaps. 22:29. The place where the angel of the Lord appeared to David, at the time when the plague was stayed, viz.; the threshing-floor of Ornan the Jebusite (chap. 21:14-18), upon Mount Moriah (2 Chron. 3:1; Gen. 22:2, 14), which was near to Mount Zion, was the place of God's habitation. Ps. 78:68, 69; 132:13, 14. And here, "like high palaces, " God's sanctuary was built. 1 Chron. 29:1.

SOLOMON AND THE PRINCES CHARGED TO BUILD THE SANCTUARY—"Now set your heart and your soul to seek the Lord your God: arise, therefore, and build ye the sanctuary of the Lord God, to bring the ark of the covenant of the Lord, and the holy vessels of God, into the house that is to be built to the name of the Lord." Chap. 22:19. "Take heed now; for the Lord hath chosen thee to build an house for the sanctuary; be strong, and do it." Chap. 28:10. Then David gave to Solomon explicit directions respecting the building of the sanctuary. Verses 11-21. A full account of the erection of this glorious sanctuary may be read in 1 Kings 6; 7; 2 Chron. 3:4. It occupied seven years and six months in [56] building, and when finished was of

61

wonderful magnificence. It principally differed from the tabernacle in being an enlargement of that plan, and in being a permanent, instead of temporary, building. The vessels of the sanctuary were also increased in size and number.

THE TABERNACLE GIVES PLACE TO THE TEMPLE.—Everything being finished in the temple of the Lord, and all Israel assembled at its dedication, we read as follows: "And they brought up the ark of the Lord, and the tabernacle of the congregation, and all the holy vessels that were in the tabernacle, even those did the priests and the Levites bring up." "And the priests brought in the ark of the covenant of the Lord unto his place, into the oracle of the house, to the most holy place, even under the wings of the cherubims." 1 Kings 8:4, 6. The tabernacle which had been at Gibeon for a long while was, as we have here read, brought up to the temple of the Lord, and the sacred vessels, and the priesthood, were transferred to that more glorious sanctuary. The ark, which had for some time been kept at Jerusalem, was carried into the most holy place in the temple. And now the habitation for the God of Jacob is complete.

GOD TAKES POSSESSION OF THE SANCTUARY.—"And it came to pass, when the priests were come out of the holy place, that the cloud filled the house of the Lord, so that the priests could not stand to minister because of the cloud;for the glory of the Lord had filled the house of the Lord. Then spake Solomon, The Lord said that he would dwell in thick darkness. I have surely built thee an house to dwell in, a settled place for [57] thee to abide in forever." 1 Kings 8:10-13. The Shekinah, or visible glory of God, which had dwelt in the tabernacle, has now passed into the temple, and that temple is thenceforward the sanctuary of the Lord God. .

THE TEMPLE WAS A PATTERN OF THE TRUE SANCTUARY.—"Then David gave to Solomon his son the porch, and of the houses thereof, and of the treasuries thereof, and of the upper chambers thereof, and of the inner parlors thereof, and of the place of the mercy seat, and the pattern of all that he had by the Spirit, of the courts of the house of the Lord, and all the chambers round about of the treasures of the house of God, and of the treasuries of the dedicated things; also for the courses of the priests and the Levites, and for all the work of the service of the house of the Lord, and for all the vessels of service in the house of the Lord." All this, said David, the Lord made me understand in writing by his hand upon me, even all the works of this pattern." 1 Chron. 28:11-13, 19. "Thou hast commanded me [Solomon] to build a temple upon thy holy mount, and an altar in the city wherein thou dwellest, are semblance of the holy tabernacle, which thou hast prepared from the beginning." Wisdom of Solomon 9:8. "The patterns of things in the heavens;" "the holy places made with hands, which are the figures of the true." Heb. 9:23, 24.

The history of the sanctuary is stated very fully in the books of Kings, and in 2 Chronicles. But we can only quote those texts in which it is called the sanctuary. In 1 Chron. 9:29, we read of "the instruments of the sanctuary, "referring either to the tabernacle or the temple. [58] In 1 Chron. 24:5, we read of "the governors of the sanctuary, "or "house of God."

The psalmist prays that God would send "help from the sanctuary." Ps. 20:2. He lifted up his hands "toward the oracle of thy sanctuary." Ps. 28:2, margin. See 1 Kings 6:19, 20. He calls upon the saints to "worship the Lord in his glorious sanctuary." Ps. 29:2, margin. He prays "to see thy power and thy glory, so as I have seen thee in the sanctuary." Ps. 63:2. He speaks of the "goings of my God, my King, in the sanctuary." Ps. 68:24, 29. In Ps. 78:54, he styles the land of Canaan "the border of the sanctuary." And in verses 68, 69, he testifies that God "built his sanctuary like high palaces" at Mount Zion in Judah. He" went into the sanctuary of God," and saw the end of the wicked. Ps. 73:17. He testifies that "thy way, O God, is in the sanctuary." Ps. 77:13. He predicts the future desolation of God's temple, or sanctuary. Ps. 74:3, 7; 79:1. In Ps. 96:6, he declares that "strength and beauty are in his sanctuary." And in verse 9, margin, he says, "O worship the Lord in the glorious sanctuary." "Lift up your hands in the sanctuary, and bless the Lord." Ps. 134:1, 2."Praise God in his sanctuary." Ps. 150:1.

From the period in which the Psalms were written, we pass down in the history of the kings of Judah to Jehoshaphat. In prayer, he states that God gave the land of Canaan to the people of Israel, "And they dwelt therein, and have built thee a sanctuary therein." 2 Chron. 20:7, 8. And inverse 9, he quotes the words used at the dedication of the temple. 1 Kings 8:33-39.

After this, we read that Uzziah, king of Judah, [59] being lifted up with pride, went into the temple to burn incense. And the priests ordered him to go out of the sanctuary. 2 Chron. 26:16-18. Still later, we read that Hezekiah offered a sin-offering for the kingdom, and for the sanctuary, and for Judah. 2 Chron. 29:21. And he called upon all Israel to yield themselves unto the Lord, and enter into his sanctuary. And he prays for those who were not cleansed according to the purification of the sanctuary. 2 Chron. 30:8, 19.

About this time, God says by Isaiah, "I have profaned the princes of the sanctuary, and have given Jacob to the curse, and Israel to reproaches." Isa. 43:28. Next, Zephaniah complains that her prophets are light and treacherous persons; her priests have polluted the sanctuary, they have done violence to the law. Zeph. 3:4.

After this, Ezekiel says, "Thou hast defiled my sanctuary." Eze. 5:11; 8:6. And in his view of the men with the slaughtering weapons, they are charged to "begin at my sanctuary." "And they began at the ancient men which were before the house." Eze. 9:9. And in chapter 23:38, 39, he says, "Moreover, this they have done unto me: they have defiled my sanctuary in the same day, and have profaned my Sabbaths. For when they had slain their children to their idols, then they came the same day into my sanctuary to profane it; and lo, thus have they done in the midst of mine house." And in chapter 24:21, God says, "I will profane my sanctuary."

GOD FORSAKES HIS SANCTUARY.—"But go ye now unto my place which is in Shiloh, where I set my name at the first, and see what I did to it for the wickedness of my people Israel. And now, because ye have done all these works, saith the [60] Lord, and I spake unto you, rising up early and speaking, but ye heard not; and I called you, but ye answered not; therefore will I do unto this house, which is called by my name, wherein ye trust, and unto the place which I gave to your fathers, as I have done to Shiloh." Jer. 7:12-14; 26:6.

What did God do to the sanctuary at Shiloh? "When God heard this, he was wroth, and greatly abhorred Israel: so that he forsook the tabernacle at Shiloh, the tent which he placed among men: and delivered his strength into captivity, and his glory into the enemy's hand:" Ps. 78:59, 61. Then when God told the people that he would do to the temple as he had done to the tabernacle at Shiloh, it was a solemn declaration that he would forsake it. Eze. 8:6. That this prediction was accomplished, we shall now show.

THE SANCTUARY DESTROYED.—"But they mocked the messengers of God, and despised his words, and misused his prophets, until the wrath of the Lord arose against his people, till there was no remedy. Therefore he brought upon them the king of the Chaldees, who slew their young men with the sword in the house of their sanctuary, and had no compassion upon young man or maiden, old man, or him that stooped for age; he gave them all into his hand. And all the vessels of the house of God, great and small, and the treasures of the house of the Lord, and the treasures of the king, and of his princes; all these he brought to Babylon. And they burnt the house of God, and brake down the wall of Jerusalem, and burnt all the palaces thereof with fire, and destroyed all the goodly vessels thereof." 2 Chron. 36:16-19.

The predictions of Asaph [61] (Ps. 74:3, 7; 79:1), of Isaiah (chapter 63:18; 64:10, 11), and of Ezekiel (chapter 24:21), were now verified. The heathen then entered "into the sanctuaries [the holies] of the Lord's house." Jer. 51:51."The heathen entered into her sanctuary, whom thou didst command that they should not enter into thy congregation." Lam. 1:10. And the Lord "cast off his altar," and "abhorred his sanctuary:" and the priest and the prophet were "slain in the sanctuary." and "the stones of the sanctuary were poured out in the top of the street." Lam. 2:7, 20; 4:1. In this time of their dispersion, and of their sanctuary's desolation, God promises to be to them "as a little sanctuary." Eze. 11:16; Isa. 8:14. The sanctuary thus destroyed, lay desolate till the reign of the kingdom of Persia. 2 Chron. 36:19-23; Ezra 1:1-3; Isa. 44:28. It was near the close of the seventy years' captivity that Daniel prayed, "Cause thy face to shine upon thy sanctuary that is desolate." Dan. 9:2, 17.

Ezekiel offers to Israel a Sanctuary

IT was fourteen years after the sanctuary had been destroyed, that God gave Ezekiel the "pattern" of another, to show to the house of Israel. Chaps. 40-48. This building consisted of two holy places. Chap. 41. And the most holy place was of the same size with that in the temple of Solomon. Verse 4; 1 Kings 6:19, 20; To this building the word sanctuary is applied in the following texts: Eze. 41:21, 23; 42:20; 43:21; 44:1, 5 verses 7, 8, refer to Solomon's temple), 9, 11, 15, 16, 27; 45:2, 3, 4, 18;47:12; 48:8, 10, 21. It was offered to the house of Israel then in captivity on this condition, that they should be [62] "ashamed" of their iniquities, and put them away. If they did this, God would cause this building to be established, and would cause "the twelve tribes" to return. Chap. 40:4;43:10, 11; 44:5-8; 47:13-33; 48.

But the house of Israel were not at all ashamed. For when the decree for Israel's restoration went forth, all Israel could go up to the land where God's abundant blessing was promised. See the decree of Cyrus. 2 Chron. 36:22, 23; Ezra 1:1-4; 7:13. But the ten tribes slighted the offer of Cyrus, as well as the promised blessings of God, and the tribes of Judah and Benjamin, with a portion of the tribe of Levi, and a few others, were all that went up. Ezra 1:5;7:7; 8:15. Thus the house of Israel rejected the gracious offer of the Lord, and slighted the inestimable blessings which God would have given them. Eze. 47; 48. Hence this sanctuary was never erected. But that this prophecy does not belong to the future reign of Christ and his saints, the following facts demonstrate:

1. The Prince that shall reign over God's people Israel, forever, is none other than Jesus Christ. There is to be but one Prince and Shepherd that shall be the King over Israel in the glorified state, and that one is Jesus. Luke 1:32, 33; Eze. 37:22, 24; Jer. 23:5, 6; Micah 5:2. But the prince here spoken of by Ezekiel is not Christ, but a poor, frail mortal. For

    1. he is commanded to offer a bullock as a sin-offering for himself. Eze. 45:22. But Jesus Christ is himself the great sin-offering for the world. 1 John 2:1, 2.

    2. He was to offer all manner of offerings for himself. Eze. 46:1-8. But Jesus Christ caused all this to "cease" at his death. Dan. [63] 9:27.

    3. God says to these princes, "Take away your exactions from my people." Eze. 45:9. But when Christ reigns, there will be nothing oppressive, for the officers will be peace, and the exactors, righteousness. Isa. 60:17-19.

    4. And this prince is to have sons and servants to whom, if he will, he may give an inheritance. But that which he gives to his servants will return to the prince in the year of Jubilee. Eze. 46:16, 17. And he is forbidden to oppress the people. Verse 18. Surely, it would be blasphemous to apply this to our Lord Jesus Christ. Hence, Ezekiel is not predicting the future reign of Christ over the house of Israel.

2. Christ says, "The children of this world [or age] marry, and are given in marriage; but they which shall be counted worthy to

obtain that world [or age], and the resurrection from the dead, neither marry, nor are given in marriage." Luke 20:35. Now hear Ezekiel: "Neither shall they [God's priests] take for their *wives* a widow, nor her that is put away; but they shall take maidens of the seed of the house of Israel, or a widow that had a priest before." Eze. 44:22. In the prediction of Christ, respecting that age or world to come, he positively affirms that there shall be no marrying or giving in marriage there; but in Ezekiel, we find the Lord's priests marrying, and have intimations even that *divorce* and *death* are not unknown! Therefore it is evident that Ezekiel does not refer to the age to come. Certain it is that had those priests been "counted worthy to obtain that world," they would not be represented as marrying in it! And this, too, in the promised land, the very heart of the future kingdom! [64]

3. And Christ adds: "Neither can they die any more; for they are equal unto the angels." Luke 20:36. And Paul testifies that at the last trump, "this mortal shall put on immortality," and death shall be swallowed up in victory. 1 Cor. 15:51-54. But Ezekiel has *deaths*, even in the families of God's priests, and they themselves defiled by attending their burials, and obliged to offer for themselves a sin-offering!! See Eze. 44:25-27. Are such persons equal to the angels? Are they where they can die no more? Surely they are not. Then it is demonstrated that Ezekiel does not refer to the world or age to come.

That the sanctuary, priesthood, and offerings, with the accompanying blessings, would have been realized in the Mosaic dispensation, had the twelve tribes of Israel accepted the proffered boon, we will now show.

1. It was to be fulfilled while circumcision was in force. Eze. 44:9. But that was abolished at the first advent. Gal. 5:2; 6:12;Col. 2:11-13.

2. It was while divorce was allowed. Eze. 44:22. But that is now done away. Matt. 5:31, 32; 19:8, 9.

3. The distinction between meats, clean and unclean, is recognized. Eze. 44:23, 31. But no such distinction is now recognized by the Bible. Rom. 14.

4. Sacrifice, offerings, burnt offerings, and sin-offerings, of bulls and goats, were then in force. Eze. 46. But they are not now acceptable to God. Heb. 10.

5. The feasts and the Jubilee were then in force. Eze. 45:21-25; 46:9, 11, 17. But they were nailed to the cross. Col. 2.

6. The Levitical priesthood was then in force. Eze. 40:46; 44:15. But the priesthood of Melchisedec, which passeth not to another, has taken its place. Heb. 5-9.

7. "The middle wall of [65] partition" then existed, as all these ordinances prove, as well as the acknowledged distinction between "the seed of the house of Israel" and the stranger. Eze. 44:22; 47:22. But it is now broken down. Eph. 2. But we leave the sanctuary offered to the twelve tribes, that we may follow the history of Judah and Benjamin.

The Sanctuary Rebuilt

CYRUS, the king of Persia, in the first year of his reign, put forth a decree for the restoration of God's sanctuary which had so long been in ruins. Ezra 1:1-4. And in this decree he not only gave permission to the whole house of Israel to go up to the city of their fathers, where God had chosen to place his name, but he actually provided help for those who needed aid to go up. And yet, ten of the twelve tribes chose to remain in their iniquity, and dwell with the heathen. But we learn in verse 5, that the chief of the fathers of Judah and Benjamin, and the priests, and the Levites, and a few others, went up. The vessels of God's house, which had been in Satan's sanctuary at Babylon (Ezra 1:7, 8; 5:14; 2 Chron. 36:7; Dan. 1:2), were delivered to them to carry up to the temple of God which they were to rebuild at Jerusalem.

And in the second year of their coming unto the house of God at Jerusalem, with Zerubbabel for their governor, and Joshua for their high priest, they laid the foundation of the temple of the Lord. Ezra 8:8, 10. After many serious hindrances, it was completed in the sixth year of Darius, its building having occupied a period of twenty years. Ezra 6:15. The decree from which the 2300 days are dated did not go forth until the seventh [66] year of the grandson of Darius. So that the sanctuary was in existence when that period commenced. Ezra 7. This temple of Zerubbabel was but the temple of Solomon rebuilt, as we may learn from Ezra 5:11, though it seems to have been larger than that building. Ezra 6:3, 4; 1 Kings 6:2. Hence it was but a continuance of the pattern of the true, which Solomon had erected. And thus we understand Paul's language in Heb. 9 as referring to these buildings, which, as a whole, make up the sanctuary of the first covenant, when he pronounces that sanctuary a figure or pattern of the true.

While Zerubbabel was building the Lord's house, the prophets Haggai and Zechariah encouraged the builders. Ezra 5:1; 6:14. Haggai promised that though it were not as rich in silver and gold as was the first house, yet the glory of this latter house should be greater than of the former, as the Desire of all nations would come to it. Hag. 2.

GOD DWELT IN THIS SANCTUARY.—"Therefore, thus saith the Lord; I am returned to Jerusalem with mercies: mine house shall be built in it, saith the Lord of hosts." Zech. 1:16." Sing and rejoice, O daughter of Zion; for lo, I come, and I will *dwell* in the midst of thee, saith the Lord." Zech. 2:10. "And whose shall swear by the temple, sweareth by it, and by him that *dwelleth* therein." Matt. 23:21.

Nehemiah calls this building the sanctuary, and declares that "we will not forsake the house of our God." Chap. 10:39. While God's house lay in ruins, Daniel prayed that God would cause his face to shine upon his sanctuary that was desolate. In answer to his prayer, the angel Gabriel is sent to inform him that at the end of 69 weeks [67] from the going forth of the decree to restore and to build Jerusalem, the Messiah would come, and would finally be cutoff. After this, the city and the sanctuary, which we have now seen rebuilt, would be destroyed, and never again be rebuilt, but left in ruins till the consummation. Dan. 9. At the end of the 69 weeks, A.D. 27, the Messiah the Prince came, and began to preach. Mark 1:15. Israel proceeded to"finish the transgression, " for which God would cut them off from being his people, by rejecting the Messiah. Dan. 9:24; John 1:11; Matt. 23:32; 1 Thess. 2:15, 16.

GOD FORSAKES THE SANCTUARY.—"O Jerusalem, Jerusalem, thou that killest the prophets, and stonest them which are sent unto thee, how often would I have gathered thy children together, even as a hen gathereth her chickens under her wings, and ye would not! *Behold your house is left unto you desolate*". Matt. 23:37, 38; Luke 13:34, 35. After uttering these words, Jesus departed from the temple, which was no longer God's habitation. And as he went out, he declared that it should be thrown down, and not one stone left upon another. Matt. 24:1, 2. And what Gabriel and Jesus had thus predicted, the Romans in a few years fulfilled, and the"worldly sanctuary" ceased to exist.

DATES.—Moses erected the sanctuary (according to the chronology in the margin), B.C. 1490. It was forsaken at Shiloh, B.C. 1141. Solomon erected the sanctuary, B.C. 1005. It was forsaken of God, B.C. 588. Rebuilt by Zerubbabel, B.C. 515. Forsaken and left desolate, A.D. 31. We have now followed the typical sanctuary to its end. And here let us pause for reflection and [68] inquiry. Why did God ordain this extraordinary arrangement? The sacrifices offered in this building could never take away sins. Why then were they instituted? The priests which here ministered were so imperfect that they had to offer for themselves. Why then was such a priesthood ordained? The building itself was but an imperfect, temporary structure, though finished to the perfection of human art. Why then was such a structure erected? Surely, God does nothing in vain, and all this is full of meaning. Nor will the student of the Bible be at a loss to answer these questions. The building itself was but a "figure of the true," a "pattern of things in the heavens." The priests which there ministered, served "unto the example and shadow of heavenly things, " and the sacrifices there offered, continually pointed forward to the great sacrifice that should be made for the sin of man. These great truths are plainly stated in Heb. 8-10. We shall now pass from the shadow to the substance

73

The Typical Sanctuary Gives Place to the True

1. The sanctuary of the first covenant ends with that covenant, and does not constitute the sanctuary of the new covenant. Heb. 9:1, 2, 8, 9; Acts 7:48, 49.
2. That sanctuary was a figure for the time then present, or for that dispensation. Heb. 9:9. That is, God did not, during the typical dispensation, lay open the true tabernacle; but gave to the people a figure or pattern of it.
3. When the work of the first tabernacle was accomplished, the way of the temple of God in Heaven was laid open. Heb. 9:8; Ps. 11:4; Jer. 17:12.
4. The typical sanctuary and the [69] carnal ordinances connected with it, were to last only till the time of reformation. And when that time arrived, Christ came, a high priest of good things to come by a greater and more perfect tabernacle. Heb. 9:9-12.
5. The rending of the veil of the earthly sanctuary at the death of our Saviour evinced that its services were finished. Matt. 27:50, 51; Mark 15:38; Luke 23:45.
6. Christ solemnly declared that it was left desolate. Matt. 23:37, 38; Luke 13:34, 35.
7. The sanctuary is connected with the host. Dan. 8:13. And the host, which is the true church, has had neither sanctuary nor priesthood

74

in Old Jerusalem the past 1800 years, but has had both in Heaven. Heb. 8:1-6.

8. While the typical sanctuary was standing, it was evidence that the way into the true sanctuary was not laid open. But when its services were abolished, the tabernacle in Heaven, of which it was a figure, took its place. Heb. 10:1-9; 9:6-12.

9. The holy places made with hands, the figures or patterns of thing sin the heavens, have been superseded by the heavenly holy places themselves. Heb. 9:23, 24.

10. The sanctuary, since the commencement of Christ's priesthood, is the true tabernacle of God in Heaven. This is plainly stated in Heb. 8:1-6.

Gabriel's Explanation
of the Sanctuary

THESE points are conclusive evidence that the worldly sanctuary of the first covenant has given place to the heavenly sanctuary of the new covenant. The typical sanctuary is forsaken, and the priesthood is transferred to the true tabernacle. Now, unless it can be changed back from the true to the type again, the old will never be rebuilt. [70]

But the most important question in the mind of the reader is this: How did Gabriel explain the sanctuary to Daniel? Did he point out to him the transition from the "figure, "or "pattern," to the "greater and more perfect tabernacle, "the true holy places? We answer, He did.

1. Gabriel explains to Daniel what portion of the 2300 days belonged to Jerusalem and the Jews. "Seventy weeks have been *cut off* upon thy people, and upon thy holy city." Dan. 9:24.—*Whiting's Translation*. Then the *whole* of the 2300 days does not belong to Old Jerusalem, the place of the earthly sanctuary, nor do they all belong to the Jews, the professed people of God in the time of the first covenant.

2. For in that period of 70 weeks, the transgression was to be finished, that is, the Jewish people were to fill up their measure of iniquity by rejecting and crucifying their Messiah, and were no longer to be his people, or host. Dan. 9:24; Matt. 23:32, 33; 21:33-43; 27:25.

76

3. Gabriel showed Daniel that the earthly sanctuary should be destroyed, shortly after their rejection of the Messiah, and never be rebuilt, but be desolate till the consummation. Dan. 9:26, 27.

4. The angel brings the new covenant to Daniel's view."He [the Messiah] shall confirm the covenant with many for one week." Dan. 9:27; Matt. 26:28.

5. He brings to Daniel's view the new covenant church, or host, viz.: the "many" with whom the covenant is confirmed. Verse 27.

6. He brings to view the new-covenant sacrifice, viz.: the cutting off of the Messiah, but not for himself. Verse 26. [71] And also the Prince, or mediator, of the new covenant. Verse 25; 11:22; Heb. 12:24.

7. He brings to Daniel's view the new-covenant sanctuary. Gabriel informed Daniel that before the close of the seventy weeks, which belonged to the earthly sanctuary, the Most Holy should be anointed. That this "Most Holy" is the true tabernacle in which the messiah is to officiate as priest, we offer the following testimony:

" 'And to anoint the Most Holy;' *kodesh kodashim*, the Holy of holies."—*Adam Clarke*. Dan. 9:24.

"Seventy weeks are determined upon thy people, and the city of thy sanctuary; that sin may be restrained, and transgression have an end; that iniquity may be expiated, and an everlasting righteousness brought in; that visions and prophecies may be sealed up, and the Holy of holies anointed."—*Houbigant's Translation* of Dan. 9:24, as cited in Clarke's Commentary.

" 'To anoint the Most Holy.' Hebrew, literally 'Holy of holies.' Heaven itself, which Christ consecrated, when he ascended and entered it, sprinkling, or consecrating, it with his own blood for us."—*Litch's Restitution*, page 89.

"And the last event of the 70 weeks, as enumerated inverse 24, was the anointing of the 'Most Holy,' or the 'Holy of holies, ' or the 'Sanctum Sanctorum.' Not that which was on earth, made with hands, but the true tabernacle, Heaven itself, into which Christ, our high priest, is for us entered. Christ was to do in the true tabernacle, in Heaven, what Moses and Aaron did in its pattern. See Heb. 6; 7; 8; 9. And Ex. 30:22-30. Also Lev. 8:10-15."—*Advent Shield*, No. 1, page 75.

The fact is plain, then, that of the vision of 2300 days concerning the sanctuary, only 490 pertained to the earthly sanctuary; and also that the iniquity of the Jewish people would in that [72] period be so far filled up that God would leave them, and the city and sanctuary would soon after be destroyed, and never be rebuilt, but left in ruins till the consummation. And it is also a fact that Gabriel did present to Daniel a view of the true tabernacle (Heb. 8:12), which about the close of the 70 weeks did take the place of the pattern. And as the ministration of the earthly tabernacle began with its anointing, so in the more excellent ministry of our great High Priest, the first act, as shown to Daniel, is the anointing of the true tabernacle, or sanctuary, of which he is a minister. Ex. 40:9-11; Lev. 8:10, 11; Num. 7:1; Dan. 9:24.

It is therefore an established fact that the worldly sanctuary of the first covenant, and the heavenly sanctuary of the new covenant, are both embraced in the vision of the 2300 days. Seventy weeks are cut off upon the earthly sanctuary, and at their termination the true tabernacle, with its anointing, its sacrifice, and its minister, is introduced. And it is interesting to notice that the transfer from the tabernacle made with hands, to the true tabernacle itself, which the Lord pitched, and not man, is placed by Gabriel at the very point where the Bible testifies that the shadow of good things to come ceased, being nailed to the cross. Col. 2:14-17. Where the offering of bulls and goats gave place to the great sacrifice (Heb. 9:11-14; 10:1-10; Ps. 40:6-8; Dan. 9:27);

where the Levitical priesthood was superseded by that of the order of Melchisedec (Heb. 5-7; Ps. 110); where the example and shadow of heavenly things was terminated by the more excellent ministry which it shadowed forth. Heb. 8:1-6. And where the holy places, [73] which were the figures of the true, were succeeded by the true holy places in Heaven. Heb. 9:23, 24. In the first part of this article, we saw that Gabriel did not explain the 2300 days and the sanctuary in Dan. 8. We now see that in Dan. 9, he explained both. With Gabriel's explanation of the sanctuary and the time, we are entirely satisfied.

The Heavenly Sanctuary

NOW of the things which we have spoken this is the sum: We have such an high priest, who is set on the right hand of the throne of the Majesty in the heavens; a minister of the sanctuary, and of the true tabernacle, which the Lord pitched, and not man." Heb. 8:1, 2. "A glorious high throne from the beginning is the place of our sanctuary." Jer. 17:12; Rev. 16:17; Ps. 11:4. "For he hath looked down from the height of his sanctuary; from Heaven did the Lord behold the earth." Ps. 102:19.

THE HEAVENLY SANCTUARY HAS TWO HOLY PLACES.— The following testimony on this point is conclusive. We gather it from the Old and New Testaments, that in the mouth of two or three witnesses every word may be established.

1. The tabernacle erected by Moses, after a forty-days' inspection of the one shown him in the mount, consisted of two holy places (Ex. 26:30-33), and is declared to be a correct pattern, or model, of that building. Ex. 25:8, 9, 40, compared with chap. 39:32-43. But if the earthly sanctuary consisted of two holy places, and the great original, from which it was copied, consisted of only one, instead of likeness, there would be perfect dissimilarity.

2. The temple was built in every respect according to the pattern which God [74] gave to David by the Spirit. 1 Chron. 28:10-19. And Solomon, in addressing God, says,"Thou hast commanded me to build a temple upon thy holy mount, and an altar in the city

80

wherein thou dwellest, a resemblance of the holy tabernacle which thou hast prepared from the beginning."Wis. Sol. 9:8. The temple was built on a larger and grander scale than the tabernacle; but its distinguishing feature, like the tabernacle, consisted in the fact that it was composed of two holy places. 1 Kings 6; 2 Chron. 3. This is clear proof that the heavenly tabernacle contains the same.

3. Paul plainly states that "the holy places [plural] made with hands" "are the figures [plural] of the true." And the tabernacle, and its vessels, are "patterns of things in the heavens." Heb. 9:23, 24. This is direct evidence that, in the greater and more perfect tabernacle, there are two holy places, even as in the "figure," "example," or "pattern."

4. The apostle actually uses the word holies (plural), in speaking of the heavenly sanctuary. The expression "holiest of all," in Heb. 9:8; 10:19, has been supposed by some to prove that Christ began to minister in the most holy place at his ascension. But the expression is not "*hagia hagion*," holy of holies, as in chapter 9:3; but is simply "*hagion*," holies. It is the same word that is rendered sanctuary in Heb. 8:2. In each of these three texts (Heb. 8:2; 9:8;10:19), Macknight renders the word,"holy places." The Douay Bible renders it "the holies." And thus we learn thatthe heavenly sanctuary consists of two "holy places."

VESSELS OF THE HEAVENLY SANCTUARY.—We have noticed particularly the vessels of the earthly sanctuary, and have cited divine testimony to show that they were patterns of the true in Heaven. [75]

This is strikingly confirmed by the fact that in the heavenly sanctuary we find the like vessels.

1. The ark of God's testament, and the cherubim. Rev. 11:19; Ps. 99:1.

2. The golden altar of incense. Rev. 8:3; 9:13.
3. The candlestick with the seven lamps. Rev. 4:5; Zech. 4:2.
4. The golden censer. Rev. 8:3. This heavenly sanctuary is called by David, Habakkuk, and John,"The temple of God in Heaven" (Ps. 11:4; Hab. 2:20; Rev. 11:19); God's "holy habitation" (Zech. 2:13; Jer. 25:30; Rev. 16:17); "greater and more perfect tabernacle" (Heb. 9:11); "the sanctuary, and true tabernacle, which the Lord pitched, and not man."Heb. 8:2.

The Treading Down
of the Sanctuary

THE agents by which the sanctuary is trodden under foot are the daily, or continual desolation, and the transgression, or abomination of desolation. Dan. 8:13;11:31; 12:11. These two desolations, as we have already seen, are paganism and papacy. It is often urged as a sufficient argument against the view of the sanctuary of God in Heaven that such a sanctuary is not susceptible of being trodden under foot. But we answer, This is not impossible, when the New Testament shows us that wicked men (apostates) tread under foot the Minister of the heavenly sanctuary, our Lord Jesus Christ. Heb. 10:29; 8:1, 2. If they can tread under foot the Minister of that sanctuary, then they can tread under foot the sanctuary itself. It is not impossible that the pagan and papal desolations should be represented as treading under foot the heavenly sanctuary, when the same vision represents the little horn as stamping upon the stars; Dan. 8:10; and when it is expressly predicted that the papal power [76] should war against the tabernacle of God in Heaven. Rev. 13:5-7. The language of this vision, that these blasphemous powers should cast down the truth to the ground, stamp upon the stars, and tread under foot the sanctuary and the host, is certainly figurative, as it would otherwise involve complete absurdities.

Let us now briefly trace the manner in which Satan has, by

paganism and papacy, trodden under foot the sanctuary of the Lord. We have already seen that he has done this by erecting rival sanctuaries, where, in the place of the only living and true God, he has established "new gods that came newly up." Deut. 32:16, 17. In the days of the Judges and of Samuel, Satan's rival sanctuary was the temple of Dagon, where the Philistines worshiped. Judges 16:23, 24. And when they had taken the ark of God from Israel, the Philistines deposited it in this temple. 1 Sam. 5. After Solomon erected a glorious sanctuary upon Mount Moriah, Jeroboam, who made Israel to sin, erected a rival sanctuary at Bethel, and thus drew away ten of the twelve tribes from the worship of the living God, to that of the golden calves. 1 Kings 12:26-33; Amos 7:13, margin. In the days of Nebuchadnezzar, the rival to the sanctuary of God was the temple of Nebuchadnezzar's god at Babylon. And into this temple he carried the vessels of the Lord's sanctuary, when he laid it desolate. Dan. 1:2; Ezra 1:7; 5:14; 2 Chron. 36:7. At a still later period, Satan established at Rome a temple or sanctuary of "all the gods." Dan. 8:11; 11:31.

After the typical sanctuary of the first covenant had given place to the true sanctuary of God, Satan baptized his pagan sanctuary and heathen rites and ceremonies, calling them Christianity. [77] Thenceforward he had at Rome a "temple of God," and in that temple, a being exalted above all that is called Godor that is worshiped. 2 Thess. 2:4. And this papal abomination has trodden under foot the holy city (Rev. 11:2; 21:2), by persuading a large portion of the human family that Rome, the place of this counterfeit temple of God, was "the holy city," or "the eternal city." And it has trodden under foot and blasphemed God's sanctuary or tabernacle (Rev. 13:6; Heb. 8:2) by calling its own sanctuary the temple of God, and by turning away the worship of them that dwell on the earth, from "the temple of God in Heaven," to the sanctuary of Satan at Rome. It has trodden under foot

84

the Son of God, the minister of the heavenly sanctuary (Heb. 10:29; 8:2), by making the pope the head of the church, instead of Jesus Christ (Eph. 5:23), and by leading men to the worship of that "son of perdition," as one able to forgive past sins, and confer the right to commit them in the future, and thus turning men from Him who alone has power on earth to forgive sins, and to pardon iniquity and transgression. Such has been the nature of the warfare which Satan has maintained against the sanctuary and the cause of God, in his vain attempts to defeat the great plan of redemption which God has been carrying forward in his sanctuary. In order to present the cleansing of the sanctuary of God in Heaven, it is necessary to notice briefly…

The Ministration and Cleansing of the Earthly Sanctuary

WE have before shown that the earthly sanctuary consisted of two holy places, and that it was a pattern of the true tabernacle of God in Heaven. We shall now present, in a brief manner, the work [78] of ministration in both those holy places, and also the work of cleansing that sanctuary, at the end of that ministration, every year, and shall prove that that ministration was the example and shadow of Christ's more excellent ministry in the true tabernacle.

The ministration in the earthly sanctuary was performed by the Levitical order of priesthood. Ex. 28; 29; Lev. 8; 9; Heb. 7. The act, preparatory to the commencement of the ministration in that earthly tabernacle, was the anointing of its two holy places, and of all its sacred vessels. Ex. 40:9; 30:26-29; Lev. 8:10. The entire work of the priests in the two holy places is summed up by Paul as follows:"Now when these things were thus ordained, the priests went always into the first tabernacle, accomplishing the service of God; but into the second went the high priest alone once every year, not without blood, which he offered for himself, and for the errors of the people." Heb. 9:6, 7. The ministration in the earthly sanctuary is thus presented before us in two grand divisions. First, the daily service in the holy place, which consisted of the regular morning and evening burnt offering (Ex. 29:38-43; Num. 28:3-8), the burning of sweet incense upon the golden altar, when the high priest lighted the lamps every morning and evening (Ex. 30:7, 8, 34-36; 31:11), the special work upon the Lord's Sabbaths, and also upon the annual sabbaths, new moons, and feasts (Num. 28:11-31; 29; Lev. 23), and beside all this, the special work for individuals as they should present their particular offerings through the year. Lev. 1-7. And second, the yearly work, in the most holy place, for the sins of the people, and for the cleansing of the sanctuary. Lev. 16. Thus each of [79] the two holy places had its appropriate work assigned. The glory of the God of Israel was manifested in both apartments. When he entered the tabernacle at the first, his glory filled both the holy places. Ex. 40:34, 35. See also 1 Kings 8:10, 11; 2 Chron. 5:13, 14; 7:1, 2. In the door of the first apartment, the Lord stood and talked with Moses. Ex. 33:9-11. In this place God promised to meet with the children of Israel, and to sanctify the tabernacle with his glory. Ex. 29:42-44; 30:36. In the holiest, also, God manifested his glory in a special manner. Ex. 25:21, 22; Lev. 16:2.

In the first apartment stood the priests in a continual course of ministration for the people. He that had sinned, brought his victim to the door of this apartment to be offered up for himself. He laid his hand upon the head of the victim to denote that his sin was transferred to it. Lev. 1-3. Then the victim was slain on account of that transgression, and his blood, bearing that sin and guilt, was carried into the sanctuary, and sprinkled upon it. Lev. 4. Thus, through the year, this ministration went forward. The sins of the people being transferred from themselves to the victims offered in sacrifice, and through the blood of the sacrifices, transferred to the sanctuary itself.

On the tenth day of the seventh month, the ministration was changed from the holy place, where it had been continued through the year, to the most holy place. Lev. 16:2, 29-34. The high priest entered the holiest with the blood of a bullock, as a sin-offering for himself. Verses 3 , 6, 11-14. He then received of the children of Israel two kids of the goats for a sin-offering. Upon these goats he cast lots; one lot for the Lord, and the other lot for the scapegoat. Verses 5, 7, 8. [80] He next proceeded to offer the goat, upon which the Lord's lot fell, as a sin-offering for the people.

We shall now show that he offered this blood for two purposes:

1.　"To make an atonement for the children of Israel, for all their sins."
2.　To cleanse or "make an atonement for the holy sanctuary."

Let us read a portion of the chapter. "Then shall he kill the goat of the sin-offering that is for the people, and bring his blood within the veil, and do with that blood as he did with the blood of the bullock, and sprinkle it upon the mercy-seat, and before the mercy-seat; and he shall make an atonement for the holy place, because of the uncleanness of the children of Israel, and because of their transgressions in all their sins; and so shall he do for the tabernacle of the congregation that remaineth among them in the midst of their uncleanness. And there shall be no man in the tabernacle of the congregation when he goeth in to make an atonement in the holy place, until he come out, and have made an atonement for himself, and for his household, and for all the congregation of Israel. And he shall go out unto the altar that is before the Lord, and make an atonement for it; and shall take of the blood of the bullock, and of the blood of the goat, and put it upon the horns of the altar round about. And he shall sprinkle of the blood upon it with his finger seven times, and cleanse it, and hallow it from the uncleanness of the children of Israel. And when he hath made an end of reconciling the holy place, and the tabernacle of the congregation, and the altar, he shall bring the live goat; and Aaron shall lay both his hands upon the head of the [81] live goat, and confess over him all

88

the iniquities of the children of Israel, and all their transgressions in all their sins, putting them upon the head of the goat, and shall send him away by the hand of a fit man into the wilderness; and the goat shall bear upon him all their iniquities unto a land not inhabited; and he shall let go the goat in the wilderness.'"''And this shall be a statute forever unto you; that in the seventh month, on the tenth day of the month, ye shall afflict your souls and do no work at all, whether it be one of your own country, or a stranger that sojourneth among you; for on that day shall the priest make an atonement for you, to cleanse you, that ye may be clean from all your sins before the Lord." "And he shall make an atonement for the holy sanctuary, and he shall make an atonement for the tabernacle of the congregation, and for the altar; and he shall make an atonement for the priests, and for all the people of the congregation. And this shall be an everlasting statute unto you, to make an atonement for the children of Israel for all their sins once a year." Verses 15-22, 29, 30, 33, 34.

We have here read several important facts.

1. On the tenth day of the seventh month the ministration was changed from the holy place to the holiest of all. Verses 2, 29-34.

2. That in the most holy place, blood was offered for the sins of the people to make an atonement for them. Verses 5, 9, 15, 17, 30, 33, 34; Heb. 9:7.

3. That the two holy places of the sanctuary, and also the altar of incense were on this day cleansed from the sins of the people, which, as we have seen, had through the year been borne into the sanctuary, and sprinkled upon it. Verses 16, 18-20, 33; Ex. 30:10.

4. That the high priest, having by blood removed the sins of the people from the sanctuary, bears them to the door of the tabernacle (Num. 18:1; Ex. 28:38) where the scapegoat stands, and putting both his hands upon the head of the goat, and [82] confessing over

him all the iniquities of the children of Israel in all their sins, he puts them upon the head of the goat, and sends him away, with all their iniquities, into a land not inhabited. Verses 5, 7-10, 20-22.

The sanctuary was thus cleansed from the sins of the people, and those sins were borne by the scapegoat from the sanctuary. The foregoing presents to our view a general outline of the ministration in the worldly sanctuary. The following scriptures show that that ministration was the example and shadow of Christ's ministry in the tabernacle in Heaven: "Now of the things which we have spoken, this is the sum: We have such an High Priest, who is set on the right hand of the throne of the Majesty in the heavens: a minister of the sanctuary, and of the true tabernacle, which the Lord pitched, and not man. For every high priest is ordained to offer gifts and sacrifices; wherefore it is of necessity that this man have somewhat also to offer. For if he were on earth, he should not be a priest, seeing that there are priests that offer gifts according to the law;who serve unto the example and shadow of heavenly things, as Moses was admonished of God when he was about to make the tabernacle; for, See (saith he) that thou make all things according to the pattern showed to thee in the mount. But now hath he obtained a more excellent ministry, by how much also he is the mediator of a better covenant, which was established upon better promises." Heb. 8:1-6;Col. 2:17; Heb. 10:1; 9:11, 12.

The facts stated in these texts are worthy of careful attention.
1. We have a High Priest in the heavens.
2. This High Priest is a minister of the sanctuary or true tabernacle.
3. As the earthly high priests were ordained to offer sacrifice [83] for sins, so it is of necessity that our High Priest should have something to offer for us in the heavenly sanctuary.
4. When upon earth, he was not a priest.
5. The ministry of the priests in that tabernacle, made after the pat-

tern of the true, was the example and shadow of Christ's more excellent ministry in the true tabernacle itself.

6. The entire typical service was a shadow of good things to come.
7. In the greater and more perfect tabernacle, Christ is a minister of these good things thus shadowed forth.

With these facts before us, let us now consider that more excellent ministry in the temple of God in Heaven.

The Ministration and Cleansing of the Heavenly Sanctuary

A T the close of the typical services, He of whom Moses in the law and prophets did write, Jesus of Nazareth, came and laid down his life for us. The death of the Lord Jesus is the dividing point between the two dispensations, as it put an end to the typical services, and was the great foundation of his work as a priest in the heavenly tabernacle. On Jesus was laid the iniquity of us all, and he bare our sins in his own body on the tree. Is a. 53:6; 1 Pet. 2:24; Heb. 9:28. He was raised from the dead for our justification, and ascended into Heaven to become a great High Priest in the presence of God for us. Rom. 4:25; Heb. 9:11, 12, 24.

The ministration in the heavenly sanctuary is performed by the Melchisedec order of priesthood, in the person of our Lord. Ps. 110; Heb. 5-8. We have already proved that the temple of God in Heaven consists of two holy places, as did the earthly tabernacle; and that the ministration in the two holy places of the worldly sanctuary was the example and shadow of Christ's ministry in the true tabernacle. But it is contended by some that Christ ministers only in the most holy place of the heavenly sanctuary. Let us examine this point.

1. His anointing the most holy place of the true [84] tabernacle, at

92

the commencement of his ministration, may be urged as proof that he ministers only in the second apartment of the heavenly sanctuary. Dan. 9:24. But this objection vanishes at once if we consider that before the Levitical priesthood began to minister in the earthly sanctuary, that entire building, the holiest as well as the holy place and all the sacred vessels, were anointed. Ex. 40:9-11; 30:23-29; Lev. 8:10; Num. 7:1. And when this anointing was accomplished, that ministration *began* in the *first* apartment. Lev. 8-10; Heb. 9:6, 7. And this order, let it be remembered, was "the example and shadow of heavenly things."

2. It has been urged by some that the text,"this man, after he had offered one sacrifice for sins, forever sat down on the right hand of God" (Heb. 10:12), forbids the idea of his ministering in the *two* holy places. But we answer, that so far as the idea of *sitting down* is concerned, it would be equally proper to represent him as *standing* on the Father's right hand. Acts 7:56. And if the Saviour is at the "right hand of the power of God" when descending from heaven, as he testifies respecting himself (Matt. 26:64; Mark 14:62; Luke 22:69), then he certainly can be at the Father's right hand, in both the holy places. But we have direct testimony here. Paul says that Christ is a "minister of the sanctuary." Heb. 8:2. That the word "*hagion*," here rendered sanctuary, is plural, no one can deny. It is literally rendered by the Douay Bible,"the holies." As translated by Macknight, Heb. 8:1, 2, reads thus: "Now of the things spoken the chief is, we have such a High Priest as became us, who sat down at the right hand of the throne of the Majesty in the heavens, a minister of the holy places, namely, of the true tabernacle, which the Lord pitched, and not man." We draw two conclusions from the foregoing:

    1. Our Lord *can* be a minister of the two holy places, and

yet be at the Father's right hand.

2. He *must* minister in both the holy places or Paul's language that he is a minister of the holies or holy places (plural), is not [85] true. An high priest that should minister simply in the holiest of all, is not a minister of the holy places.

3. But another argument to prove that Christ ministers only in the most holy place, has been urged by some, from the following texts: "The Holy Ghost this signifying, that the way into the holiest of all was not yet made manifest, while as the first tabernacle was yet standing." Heb. 9:8."Having, therefore, brethren, boldness to enter into the holiest by the blood of Jesus." Chap. 10:19. But, as has been before remarked, the word rendered "holiest of all" is the same that is rendered "sanctuary" in chapter 8:2, and is not "*hagia hagion*," holy of holies, as in chapter 9:3, but is simply "hagion," holies, plural. The rendering of Macknight, which correctly translates the word in the plural, removes all difficulty. He translates these two texts as follows: "The Holy Ghost signifying this, that the way of the holy places was not yet laid open while the first tabernacle still standeth." "Well, then, brethren, having boldness in the entrance of the holy places, by the blood of Jesus." These texts, therefore, do not favor the doctrine that Christ is a minister of only one of the holy places. With a literal rendering of the word, giving it in the plural in our language, just as it was written by Paul, the objection to Christ's ministration in the two holy places of the heavenly sanctuary is entirely removed. The way into the holy places of the heavenly sanctuary was not laid open while the ministration in the earthly tabernacle continued, but when that ministration was abolished, the way of the heavenly holy places was laid open, and we have boldness to enter by faith, where our High Priest is ministering for us.

94

It may be proper to add, that the phrase rendered,"into the holy place," in Heb. 9:12, 25, and "into the sanctuary," in chapter 13:11, is the same that in chapter 9:24 is literally rendered in the plural,"into the holy places." Macknight renders them all in the plural. Then the heavenly tabernacle, where our Lord Jesus Christ ministers, is composed of holy places, as [86] really as was its pattern or image, the earthly tabernacle; and our great High Priest is a minister of those holy places while at the Father's right hand.

Let us now examine those scriptures which present our Lord's position and ministry in the tabernacle in heaven. In vision at Patmos, the beloved disciple has a view of the temple of God, the heavenly sanctuary. A door was opened *in Heaven*. This must be the door of the heavenly tabernacle, for it disclosed to John's view the throne of God, which was in that temple. Rev. 4:1, 2; 16:17; Jer. 17:12. It must be the door of the first apartment, for that of the second apartment (which discloses the ark containing the commandments) is not opened until the sounding of the seventh angel. Rev. 11:19. And the view, that John was looking into the first apartment of the heavenly sanctuary, when he saw the Lord Jesus take the book from the hand of him that sat upon the throne, is strikingly confirmed by what he saw before the throne. He testifies that "there were seven lamps of fire burning before the throne, which are the seven spirits of God." Rev. 4:5; Zech. 4:2. He also saw the golden altar of incense before the throne, and witnessed the ministration at that altar with the golden censer. Rev. 8:3. In the earthly tabernacle, which was the pattern of things in the heavens, the golden candlestick, with its seven lamps, and the golden altar of incense, were both represented, and by God's express direction, placed in the first apartment. Num. 8:2-4; Heb. 9:2; Lev. 24:2-4. Ex. 40:24-27. The scene of this vision is the first apartment of the heavenly sanctuary. Here it was that John saw the Lord Jesus. Rev. 5:6-8.

Let us read Isaiah's description of this place. "In the year that king Uzziah died, I saw, also, the Lord sitting upon a throne, high and lifted up, and his train filled the temple. Above it stood the seraphim: each one had six wings; with twain he covered his face, and with twain he covered his feet, and with twain he did fly. And one cried unto another, and said, Holy, holy, holy, is the Lord of Hosts: the whole earth is full of [87] his glory. And the posts of the door moved at the voice of him that cried, and the house was filled with smoke. Then said I, Woe is me! for I am undone; because I am a man of unclean lips, and I dwell in the midst of a people of unclean lips; for mine eyes have seen the King, the Lord of Hosts. Then flew one of the seraphim unto me, having a live coal in his hand, which he had taken with the tongs from off the altar" (Isa. 6:1-6).

That this was a view of the heavenly tabernacle, and not of the temple at Jerusalem, may be proved by comparing John 12:39-41, with Isa. 6:8-10. Words written by Isaiah, while looking into the temple of God, are quoted by John, with the declaration that Isaiah spake them while beholding Christ's glory. That John and Isaiah both beheld the same place is evident; both beheld the throne of God, and him that sits upon it (Isa. 6:1; Rev. 4:2); both beheld the living beings with six wings (Isa. 6:2; Rev. 4:8); and both beheld the golden altar before the throne. Isa. 6:6; Rev. 8:3;9:13. That John and Isaiah both saw our Lord Jesus Christ, we have already proved. And the scene of their visions was in the first apartment of the heavenly sanctuary, the place of the golden candlestick with its seven lamps, and the golden altar of incense. And in this apartment our High Priest commenced his ministration, like the priests in the example and shadow of heavenly things. In the shadow, each part of the work was many times repeated; but in the substance, each part is fulfilled once for all. Once for all, our Sacrifice is slain (Rom. 6:9, 10; Heb. 9:25-28); and once for all our

96

High Priest appears in each of the holy places. Heb. 9:11, 12, 24, 25. Hence, our Lord must continue his ministration in the first apartment until the period arrives for his ministration within the second veil, before the ark of God's testament.

The sins of the world were laid upon the Lord Jesus, and he died for those sins according to the Scriptures. The blood of the Lamb of God, which was shed for our [88] transgressions of God's law, is that by which our High Priest enters the heavenly sanctuary (Heb. 9:12), and which, as our advocate, he offers for us in that sanctuary. Heb. 12:24; 1 Pet. 1:2; 1 John 2:1, 2. His great work, which began with the act of bearing the sins of the world at his death, he here carries forward by pleading the cause of penitent sinners, and presenting for them his blood, which had been shed as the great sacrifice for the sins of the world. The work in the earthly sanctuary was essentially the same thing. The sins were there laid upon the victim, which was then slain. The blood of that sacrifice, bearing that guilt, was sprinkled in the sanctuary to make reconciliation for the sinner. Lev. 4:4-6.

And thus, in the shadow of heavenly things, we see the guilt of the people transferred to the sanctuary itself. This can be easily understood. And it is a plain fact that its great design was to give an example of heavenly things. As the sin of him who came to God through the offering of blood by the high priest, was, through that blood, transferred to the sanctuary itself, so it is in the substance. He who bore our sins at his death, offers for us his blood in the heavenly sanctuary. But when he comes again, he is "without sin" (Heb. 9:28); his great work for the removal of sin is fully completed before he comes again. We now inquire respecting the removal of the sins of the church, or host, from the sanctuary. We have seen that only 490 of the 2300 years belonged to the earthly sanctuary, and that the remaining 1810 years belong to the true sanctuary, which Gabriel introduces to

Daniel in his explanation in chapter 9; consequently, the sanctuary to be cleansed from the sins of the church, or host, at the end of the 2300 years, is the heavenly sanctuary. We have also examined those portions of the Bible that explain how and why the earthly sanctuary was cleansed, and have seen that that cleansing was accomplished, not by fire, but by blood. We have seen that that work was ordained for the express purpose of shadowing forth the work in the heavenly sanctuary. And we have also seen that the sins of those who come to God through [89] our great High Priest are communicated to the sanctuary as was the case in the type. But we are not left without direct testimony on this important point. The apostle Paul states the fact of the cleansing of the earthly and the heavenly sanctuaries, and plainly affirms that the latter must be cleansed for the same reason that the former had been. He speaks as follows: "And almost all things are by the law purged with blood; and without shedding of blood is no remission. It was therefore necessary that the patterns of things in the heavens should be purified with these; but the heavenly things themselves with better sacrifices than these. For Christ is not entered into the holy places made with hands, which are the figures of the true; but into Heaven itself, now to appear in the presence of God for us." Heb. 9:22-24. Two important facts are stated in this portion of Scripture.

1. The earthly sanctuary was cleansed by blood.
2. The heavenly sanctuary must be cleansed by better sacrifice, that is, by the blood of Christ. It is plain, then, that the idea of cleansing the sanctuary by fire has no support in the Bible.

These words, as rendered by Macknight, are very clear:"And almost all things, according to the law, are cleansed with blood, and without the shedding of blood, there is nor emission. There was a necessity, therefore, that there presentations indeed of the holy places

98

in the heavens should be cleansed by these sacrifices; but the heavenly holy places themselves, by sacrifices better than these. Therefore Christ hath not entered into the holy places made with hands; the images of the true holy places; but into heaven itself, now to appear before the face of God, on our account." Heb. 9:22-24. Then the fact of the cleansing of the heavenly sanctuary is plainly taught by the apostle Paul in his commentary on the typical system. And this great truth, plainly stated, is worthy of lasting remembrance.

By many, the idea of the cleansing of the heavenly sanctuary will be treated with scorn,"because," say they,"there is nothing in Heaven to be cleansed." Such overlook the fact that the holy of holies, where God [90] manifested his glory, and which no one but the High Priest could enter, was, according to the law, to be cleansed, because the sins of the people were borne into it by the blood of sin-offering. Lev. 16. And they overlook the fact that Paul plainly testifies that the heavenly sanctuary must be cleansed for the same reason. Heb. 9:23, 24. See also Col. 1:20. It was unclean in this sense only: the sins of men had been borne into it through the blood of sin offering, and they must be removed. This fact can be grasped by every mind.

The work of cleansing the sanctuary changes the ministration from the holy place to the holiest of all. Lev. 16; Heb. 9:6, 7; Rev. 11:19. As the ministration in the holy place of the temple in heaven began immediately after the end of the typical system, at the close of the sixty-nine and a half weeks (Dan. 9:27), so the ministration in the holiest of all, in the heavenly sanctuary, begins with the termination of the 2300 days. Then our High Priest enters the holiest to cleanse the sanctuary. The termination of this great period marks the commencement of the ministration of the Lord Jesus in the holiest of all. This work, as presented in the type, we have already seen was for a twofold purpose, viz.: the forgiveness of iniquity, and the cleansing of the sanctuary. And this great work our Lord accomplishes with his own blood; whether by the actual presentation of it, or by virtue of its merits, we need not stop to inquire.

No one can fail to perceive that this event, the cleansing of the sanctuary, is one of infinite importance. This accomplishes the great work of the Messiah in the tabernacle in heaven, and renders it complete. The work of cleansing the sanctuary is succeeded by the act of placing the sins, thus removed upon the head of the scapegoat, to be borne away forever from the sanctuary. The work of our High Priest for the sins of the world will then be completed, and he be ready to appear "without sin unto salvation." The act of placing the sins upon the head of the scapegoat, in the type has already been noticed. Lev. 16:5, 7-10, [91] 20-22.

The following valuable remarks on this important point are from the pen of O.R.L. Crozier, written in 1846:

> "THE SCAPEGOAT.—The next event of that day, after the sanctuary was cleansed, was the putting of all the iniquities and transgressions of the children of Israel upon the scapegoat, and sending him away into a land not inhabited, or of separation. It is supposed by almost everyone that this goat typified Christ in some of his offices, and that the type was fulfilled at the first advent. From this opinion I must differ, because,
>
> 1. That goat was not sent away till after the high priest had *made an end* of cleansing the sanctuary. Lev. 16:20, 21. Hence that event cannot meet its antitype till after the end of the 2300 days.
> 2. It was sent away from Israel into the wilderness, a land not inhabited, to receive them. If our blessed Saviour is its antitype, he also must be sent away, not his body alone, but soul and body (for the goat was sent away alive), from, not to, nor into, his people; neither into Heaven, for that is not a wilderness, or land not inhabited.

100

3. It received and retained all the iniquities of Israel; but when Christ appears the second time, he will be 'without sin.'

4. The goat received the iniquities from the hands of the priest, and he *sent it away*. As Christ is the priest, the goat must be something else besides himself which he can *send away.*

5. This was one of two goats, chosen for that day, of which one was the Lord's , and was offered for a sin-offering; but the other was not called the Lord's neither offered as a sacrifice. Its only office was to receive the iniquities from the priest, after he had cleansed the sanctuary from them, and bear them into a land not inhabited, leaving the sanctuary, priest, and people, behind, and free from their iniquities. Lev. 16:7-10, 22.

6. The Hebrew name of the scapegoat, as will be seen from the margin of verse 8, is Azazel. On this verse, Wm. Jenks, in his Comp. Com. has the following remarks: 'Scapegoat. See different opinions in Bochart. Spencer, after the *oldest* opinion of the Hebrews and Christians, thinks Azazel is the name of the devil; and so Rosen-muller, whom see. The Syriac has Azzail the angel (strong one) who revolted.'

7. At the appearing of Christ, as taught in Rev. 20, Satan is to be bound and cast into the bottomless pit, which act and place are significantly symbolized by the ancient high priest sending the scapegoat into a separate and un-inhabited wilderness.

8. Thus we have the scripture, the definition of the name in two ancient languages, both spoken at the same time, and the oldest opinion of the Christians in favor of re-garding the scapegoat as a type of Satan. In the common use of the term, men always associate [92] it with some-thing mean, calling refugees from justice, scapegoats. Ignorance of the law and its meaning is the only possible origin that can be assigned for the opinion that the scape-goat was a type of Christ.

"Because it is said, 'The goat shall bear upon him all their iniquities into a land not inhabited' [Lev. 16:22], and John said, 'Behold the Lamb of God, that taketh[margin,

101

beareth] away the sin of the world, ' it is concluded without further thought that the former was the type of the latter. But a little attention to the law will show that the sins were borne from the people by the priest, and from the priest by the goat.

1.   They are imparted to the victim.
2.   The priest bore them in its blood to the sanctuary.
3.   After cleansing it from them, on the tenth day of the seventh month, he bore them to the scapegoat.
4.   The goat finally bore them away beyond the camp of Israel to the wilderness.

"This was the legal process, and when fulfilled, the author of sins will have received them back again (but the ungodly will bear their own sins), and his head will have been bruised by the seed of the woman; 'the strong man armed' will have been bound by a stronger than he, and his house (the grave) spoiled of its goods, the saints. Matt. 12:29; Luke 11:21, 22.

The great work of atonement is now complete, and the work of our Lord as priest, accomplished. The sins of those who have obtained pardon through the great sin-offering, are, at the close of our Lord's work in the holy places, blotted out (Acts 3:19), and being then transferred to the scapegoat, are borne away from the sanctuary and host forever, and rest upon the head of their author, the devil.

The Azazel, or antitypical scapegoat, will then have received the sins of those who have been pardoned in the sanctuary, and in the lake of fire will suffer for the sins which he has instigated. God's people, the host, will then be free forever from their iniquity. "He that is unjust, let him be unjust still; and he which is filthy, let him be filthy still; and he that is righteous, let him be righteous still; and he that is holy, let him be holy still. And behold, I come quickly; and my reward is with me, to give every man according as his work shall be," Rev. 23:11, 12. "And to you, who are troubled, rest with us, when the Lord Jesus shall be revealed from heaven with his mighty angels, in flaming fire, taking vengeance on *them* [93] that know not God, and that *obey not* the gospel of our Lord Jesus Christ." 2 Thess. 1:7, 8.

102

Cause of Our Disappointment

WHY were those disappointed who looked for Jesus in 1844? This important question, we believe, can be answered in the most satisfactory manner. Our disappointment did not arise from mistaking the commencement of the 70 weeks. The argument by which the original date is sustained, is, as we have seen, invulnerable. Nor did our disappointment arise from a mistake in believing that the 70 weeks form a part of the 2300 days; for every part of that argument, as we have shown, still stands good. These two points being susceptible of the clearest proof, we were not mistaken in believing that the 2300 days would terminate in the seventh Jewish month, 1844. Neither did our disappointment arise from believing that at the end of the 2300 days the work of cleansing the sanctuary would take place; for it is plainly stated,"Unto 2300 days; then shall the sanctuary be cleansed."

But when we said that this earth, or a part of this earth, was the sanctuary, and that Christ must descend from Heaven at the end of the 2300 days, to purify the earth by fire, we looked for that which the Bible did not warrant us to expect. Here was the cause of our disappointment. For we have seen that there is no scriptural authority to support the view that any part of the earth is the sanctuary, or that the burning of the earth, and the melting of the elements (2 Pet. 3), is the cleansing of the sanctuary. By a multitude of witnesses, we have proved that the tabernacle of God is the sanctuary to be cleansed, and that its cleansing is a work performed in that sanctuary, with blood, and not with fire. Our disappointment, then, arose from a misunderstanding of the work to transpire at the end of the days.

Our evidence established two points:

1. The fact that the sanctuary should be cleansed at the end of the 2300 days, and that they should terminate in the seventh month, 1844.

2. The types in the example and shadow of heavenly things, set before us the work of the high priest in the seventh month, viz.: his act of passing from the holy place to the holiest of all, to cleanse the sanctuary.

We reasoned, that as the paschal lamb, which was slain on the fourteenth day of the first month, met its antitype in the death of the Lamb of God, on that day (Ex. 12:3-6, 46; 1 Cor. 5:7; John 18:23; 19:36); and the offering of the first-fruits on the sixteenth day of that month, met its antitype in the resurrection of Christ, on that day, the first fruits of them that slept (Lev. 28:10, 15; 1 Cor. 15:20, 23; Matt. 28:1, 2); and the feast of Pentecost met its antitype on the day of its [94] occurrence (Lev. 28:15-21; Acts 2:1, 2); so the cleansing of the sanctuary in the seventh month (Lev. 16); at that time in the year when the 2300 days would end, we believed would meet its antitype at the end of that period.

Could we then have understood the subject of the heavenly sanctuary, our disappointment would have been avoided. Our evidence did not prove that our High Priest would descend from the holy place of the heavenly sanctuary, in flaming fire to burn the earth, at the end of the 2300 days; but so far from this, it did prove that he must, at that time, enter within the second veil, to minister for us before the ark of God's testament, and to cleanse the sanctuary. Dan. 8:14;

Heb. 9:23, 24. Such has been the position of our High Priest since the end of the days, and this is the reason that we did not behold our King in 1844. He had then ministered in only one of the holy places, and the termination of the 2300 days marked the commencement of his ministration in the other. For believing in a literal sanctuary in Heaven, consisting of two real holy places, and that our High Priest, while at the father's right hand, is a minister of *both* these holy places, we are ranked as spiritualizers, by our enemies. From this unjust charge, we appeal to the Judge of all the earth, who will do right.

When John, who saw the door of the first apartment of the heavenly tabernacle opened at the commencement of Christ's ministry, was carried in vision down the stream of time to"the days of the voice of the seventh angel," he saw the most holy place of God's temple opened. "And the temple of God was opened in heaven, and there were seen in his temple the ark of his testament; and there were lightnings, and voices, and thunderings, and an earthquake, and great hail." Rev. 11:19. here, by the ark of God's testament, is where our high priest ministers, since the close of the 2300 days. To this *open door* in the heavenly sanctuary (Rev. 8:7, 8; Is a. 22:22-25), we invite those to come for pardon and salvation, who have not sinned away the day of grace. Our High Priest stands by the MERCY-SEAT (the top of the ark), and here he offers his blood, not merely for the cleansing of the sanctuary, but also for the pardon of iniquity and transgression. But while we call men to this open door, and point them to the blood of Christ, offered for us at the mercy-seat, we would remind them of the LAW OF GOD beneath that mercy-seat, which made the death of God's beloved Son necessary in order that guilty man might be pardoned. That ark contains God's commandments, and he that would receive the blessing of God, at the hand of our High Priest, must keep the commandments contained in the ark, before which he ministers.

105

Many affirm that God has abolished his law; but this is so far from the truth, that [95] that law occupies the choicest place in Heaven. It is that"justice and judgment," which are the habitation of God's throne. Ps. 89:14; 97:2; Rev. 11:19.

Two of the messages of Rev. 14, had been given prior to the end of the 2300 days in 1844, as nearly all Advent believers once admitted. The third angel, with the commandments of God and the faith of Jesus, gives the last message of mercy, while our High Priest ministers for us before the ark containing the commandments. While he is thus ministering, the host, or church, are waiting the completion of the great work, the putting away of their sins. They are "in the last end of the indignation," which occupies a space of time, as is evident from Dan. 8:19.

The close of the third angel's message is marked by the Son of Man taking his position upon the white cloud. Rev. 14:9-14. The last message of mercy will then have closed, and there will be no intercessor between an offended God and guilty, offending man. The angels with the vials of God's wrath, who are now stayed by the ministration of our great High Priest, will then come out of the temple of God, and pour out the vials of unmixed wrath upon the heads of all the wicked. The plagues, the earthquake, and the great hail,"every stone about the weight of a talent," will follow; the enemies of God will be destroyed, and the little horn will be broken without hand. Rev. 15;16; 11:19;Dan. 12:1; 8:25. The sanctuary and the host will then be vindicated, and all opposing power overwhelmed in irretrievable ruin.

Beyond this time of trouble, such as never was, the scenes of the earth made new rise before us. In the midst of that paradise of God, where his saints will ever remain, we behold his glorious sanctuary (Eze. 37; Rev. 21:1-4); and here we leave it, content, if we may be of the number who shall serve God in that temple, forever and ever. Rev. 7:13-15. The prophetic views of Moses and of Nathan, respecting God's sanctuary, will then be fully realized;the Lord will reign forever and ever, and Israel will be planted, to be removed no more. Ex. 15; 2 Sam. 7.

Reader, would you escape the things that are coming on the earth? The warning voice of the third angel points out the way. Know for yourself that you have a personal interest in that work which our High Priest is consummating before the ark of God's testament, and when he shall come again, it will be without sin unto your salvation. We entreat you, heed not the voice of those who break the commandment, and teach men so; for they will soon receive their reward; but rather unite with those who teach and keep them, and you will have life eternal, and free admittance through the gates into the holy city. [96]

We invite you to view the complete
selection of titles we publish at:

www.TEACHServices.com

Scan with your mobile
device to go directly
to our website.

Please write or email us your praises, reactions, or
thoughts about this or any other book we publish at:

TEACH Services, Inc.
P U B L I S H I N G
www.TEACHServices.com

P.O. Box 954
Ringgold, GA 30736

info@TEACHServices.com

TEACH Services, Inc., titles may be purchased in bulk for
educational, business, fund-raising, or sales promotional use.
For information, please e-mail:

BulkSales@TEACHServices.com

Finally, if you are interested in seeing
your own book in print, please contact us at

publishing@TEACHServices.com

We would be happy to review your manuscript for free.